ATONEMENT FOR IWO

By
Lester Taube

Bookman LLC
Publishing & Marketing
Providing Quality, Professional
Author Services
www.bookmanmarketing.com

ISBN: 1-59453-382-2

DEDICATION

To those who paid for this small piece of land.

Other Novels by Lester Taube

The Grabbers
(The Diamond Boomerang)
Peter Krimsov
Myer For Hire
The Cossack Cowboy

Atonement for Iwo

PROLOGUE

1945

First Lieutenant Keith Masters neared the edge of the cliff and raised his hand for the patrol to stop. The soldiers promptly sank to the ground with sighs of relief. There was a soft breeze flowing in from the sea, and the sun was bright. To the left were the sounds of machine guns. The marines were still reducing Japanese strong points. Mopping up an island was always a dirty and fatiguing job, especially when the holdouts knew it was a lost cause.

Masters took off his helmet, wiped his sweaty forehead, squatted, and drew out a pack of cigarettes from a pocket sewn on the sleeve of his fatigue shirt. Behind him, in the distance, loomed the sharp peak of Mount Suribachi, Iwo Jima.

"Where to now?" asked Sergeant Schneider, as he sat down beside the officer.

Masters peered over the edge of the cliff down to the sands below, a narrow ribbon of white running between the precipice and the calm sea. "We'll move along the beach," he said, squinting into the harsh glare of the sun bouncing off the water. "We haven't searched it for a few days now."

Sergeant Schneider frowned, his broad face drawing down into an expression of unease. "I don't like that area," he said, in his dull, Midwestern drawl. "Lieutenant Howard found a gang of duds out there the last time through."

"Tough shit," said Masters. He did not care much for Schneider. The beefy sergeant was more suited for rear echelon duty than leading combat patrols. He wanted the glory without being handed the bill. But he had been assigned as a squad leader in his platoon, and Masters was not about to let him sit on his ass back in the perimeter. He threw away his half-smoked cigarette and rose, a tense, wiry man of twenty-five, medium height, with cropped brown hair and light blue eyes. "Let's get going," he called to the men.

He led the way to a cut in the cliff and started downward, turning to hang from a projection before dropping to a ledge below. Slowly, carefully, he found the safest way down for the patrol. Soon the men had descended the fifty-foot cliff-face to the beach.

"Single file," he ordered, motioning for one of the squad to take the point position. The men moved forward cautiously along the forty yard wide strip of sand, their eyes glued upward at the cliff, searching for occupied caves.

After about a hundred yards, Masters stopped to look closely at a small opening halfway up the steep rock. Without turning his head, he said to Schneider, who was directly behind, "There's sure as hell a Nip in that hole. I bet that's where the goddamn shot came from last time through."

Schneider focused his binoculars on the opening, which was about thirty feet up. "It's pretty small," he commented.

"Those bastards don't need a helluva lot to get in," growled Masters. "And those holes open into caves big enough to hide a truck. Pass the word to Stapler in the rear to keep his eye on it as we go by. At the first sign of movement, start shooting."

He felt a chill run down his spine as he passed the opening. At each step or two he shifted quickly from one side to the other. During the last patrol through here, about four days ago, at this very point, a bullet had kicked up sand at his feet, fired from one of the dozen caves in the cliff-face.

The patrol continued its search to the northernmost tip of the island. Directly ahead, an arm of the cliff curved into the sea, bringing the ribbon of sand to an end. Masters halted the twelve-man patrol for another break.

The officer squatted and lit a cigarette. He watched Gorman, one of the recent replacements, walk up to the ocean's edge to look for shells. Gorman stepped into the water to grab at one of them as the calm waves receded.

Goddamn fool, thought Masters. He'll ruin his boots sure as hell.

Gorman waded to the end of the cliff, which projected twenty feet or so into the sea, and looked around it. Suddenly he stiffened, whirled about, and began rushing back to the beach. Masters straightened up.

"Japs!" he shouted. "Just around the bend!" The safety locks of the soldiers' weapons were pushed to the 'fire' position.

Motioning to his men to wait, Masters waded out into the water. It was well up to his thighs when he reached the point. Slowly he edged his head around. The cliff fell back sharply to disclose a shallow cave at its base, its mouth barricaded by a two-foot high wall of stone.

Masters gripped his Thompson submachine gun more tightly as he stepped around the point.

A Japanese soldier was squatting off to one side by the water's edge, pants down to relieve himself, his eyes fastened on the sand. Two more soldiers were seated behind the stone wall, speaking to each other.

Masters took three slow steps forward. He tried desperately to remember how to say surrender in Japanese, but the words eluded him. At the same time, his brain registered the danger of being unable to see the hands of the enemy behind the wall.

Suddenly, the squatting man looked up! His eyes opened wide in disbelief. Masters fired at once. Three bullets bored into the Japanese's chest, driving him onto his back. His legs kicked violently in his death throes.

The two Japanese leaning against the wall froze. Masters shot them in quick succession. A movement next to the enemy caught his eye! A fourth Japanese, lying down out of sight, abruptly sat up! A burst sent him sprawling over the others.

Masters advanced warily to the beach, his weapon at the ready. The first Japanese shot was lying motionless, his eyes wide open, three blue holes over his heart. The officer continued on to the cave. The two he had next shot were also dead, sprawled in a tangle. The fourth was stirring, feebly trying to turn.

Sergeant Schneider came hurrying up to his side. "That one's still alive!" he said hoarsely. He snapped his rifle to his shoulder, aimed deliberately, then shot the wounded Japanese directly in the head.

"What the goddamn hell did you do that for?" growled Masters.

"He was still moving!" said Schneider, his voice rising.

"I saw it, you asshole. Maybe I wanted him alive." In disgust, he turned away. The patrol had come around the point and was wading up to the beach. "Pull them out," ordered the officer. With apparent eagerness, the soldiers dragged the bodies from the cave and began to search them for souvenirs.

The last one shot was a sergeant, a saber hooked to his belt.

"It's mine," said Schneider. "I killed him." The men looked up at Masters, leaning against the cave, smoking.

"Horseshit, it's yours," snapped Sergeant Yeager. "Look at his chest." He pointed to three holes grouped there, just off center. "They're from the Lieutenant's tommy gun. You blew off that Nip's head after he was dead."

"He was still moving," shouted Schneider. He turned to Masters. "Wasn't he, Lieutenant?"

The officer straightened up and spat. "It goes into the pot, Sergeant," he said sharply. We walked over to inspect the souvenirs lying by the bodies. The rule was three choices for the man who killed - the remainder to be distributed by drawing lots.

He stopped at the side of the Japanese sergeant and gazed down at the face which had been disfigured by the rifle bullet tearing through his head. The crown had cracked open like a ripe melon. Beside him was a wallet. Masters picked it up. Next to the wallet was a thousand-stitch belt with a coin sewn in the middle - a good luck charm. He picked that up, too.

"Divide the rest," he ordered.

Then he turned and waded into the sea, around the edge, away from this place of death.

CHAPTER 1

June, 1965

Keith Masters jabbed his thumb on the doorbell, then, without waiting for a call to enter, opened the door and strode through the dimly-lit hallway to the dining room at the rear of the house. A large, round table stood in the center of the room with a matching buffet off to one side.

"Hi, Mamie," he greeted the fat Negress seated in front of a television set. He made his way around the table to the buffet and picked up an envelope marked 'Metropolitan Life Insurance Company'. Inside were a receipt book and three one dollar bills. He marked down two weeks' payment in the book, then opened his heavy debit book to record it there.

Mamie waited for a commercial before turning away from the television set. "Hi there, Mistah Masters. Where's Mistah Bronsky?"

Masters grinned. "He's sick. He got the clap from screwing all you girls on the debit."

The fat woman shook with laughter. "Ah swear, Mistah Masters, Ah sure do miss you on the debit."

Masters pocketed the three dollars, fired up a cigarette, and eyed her. "How's everything going, Mamie?"

She pursed her lips. "Pretty good, considerin' how sick Ah've been the last five years." She cocked her head. "What you doin' now. Ain't seen you fur a long time."

"I'm out with the boys all the time. Being an assistant manager is just a crock of crap."

The woman, torn between wanting to watch her daily show or asking a question, dragged her eyes away to look back at Masters. "You tell that Mistah Bronsky Ah wants to know what's goin' on with that policy fur Lily."

Masters shook his head. "Hasn't he refunded the money?"

"What you mean, refunded the money?"

"For Christ's sake, Mamie, I've told you a dozen times not to try grabbing a big policy for Lily. I told you to buy it bit-by-bit, quarter by quarter. Who dreamed up that ten dollar a month shit?"

"Mistah Bronsky said he'd get it through."

Masters shook his head again. "Well, he didn't get it through. It was rejected, just like the other three applications over the last five years."

"What fur they always rejectin' Lily?"

"Oh, Jesus Christ, Mamie, you know better than that. There isn't a guy in town who hasn't screwed Lily. The Company doesn't mind you having a piece of ass now and then, but when you make a business of it…"

Mamie's eyes narrowed. "That ain't true, and you know it."

He leaned over the table. "Name one guy who hasn't fucked her?"

Her eyes narrowed further, then a twinkle came into them. "You!" she shouted, her heavy breasts heaving with laughter.

Master grinned as he closed the debit book. "I'm holding out for you, baby," he chuckled, starting out of the house. Behind him, the room shook from her mirth.

On the street, he looked at his watch, surprised to see it was almost noon. He glanced at his route sheet. The next collection was in the Italian neighborhood. He walked the four blocks to where his car was parked and climbed inside. He turned the key three times before the motor caught.

Goddamn car, he muttered, eyeing the 1958 Chevrolet with distaste. If I ever get those fucking bills paid off, the first thing I'll do is drop this heap in the junkyard.

He drove out of the Negro area to a drug store and sat at the counter to eat a ham sandwich. Thirty minutes later, he was on his way to the Italian section. He parked the car, got out, and opened the debit book to the route card. The first house to collect from was halfway down the block, on the other side of the street. He stepped off the curb.

(God!) his mind screamed, as a fiery slash of pain ripped at his chest! His mouth opened wide to gasp for breath.

(God!) He fell to his knees, the debit book sliding under the car.

(Help!) his mind cried out. Then he crumpled to the ground.

Mr. and Mrs. Elvino, seated on their porch across the street, saw him fall. The woman grasped her husband's arm. "Tony, that'sa Mister Masters. Quick!"

The old Italian limped down the steps and across to the stricken man. He kneeled and rolled him over, then turned startled eyes towards his wife.

"He'sa dead!" he shouted. "Calla de police."

(God, oh God! Stop the pain!) Master's mind shrieked.

Angelo Foretti, picking his teeth, came out of the house directly behind them. He took one look and ran down the steps.

"What's the matter, Tony?"

"He'sa dead."

Angelo kneeled to peer into the pale, clammy face. "He sure is. Who is he?"

"Insurant man, from de Metropolitan."

(Stop! Please stop!)

"He had a heart attack," explained Foretti. "I saw the same thing with my Aunt Mary. Bang! Just like that. One minute she's reaching across the table to pour some wine, and the next minute she's lying over all the food. I thought Mom would have a fit."

(God!) the scream started. Then a merciful curtain of darkness cut it off.

A thin, colorless ray of light bored into the brain cell. The cell quivered under the violent impact, then passed on the vibration to the cells surrounding it. The motion spread out like a circular ripple triggered by a pebble dropped into a motionless pool as it rolled faster and faster in its rush to sensibility.

"Can you hear me, Mr. Masters?"

Masters' eyes flickered, his head turned slowly to one side, his face muscles relaxed, his shallow breathing grew more steady.

"I think he'll be all right," said the cardiologist as he closed the flap of the oxygen tent. He turned to the nurse standing at the foot of the bed. "Keep him under constant observation and call me the moment he stirs." He left the room with a younger doctor trailing behind. "That was a close one," he commented in the hallway. "Imagine, a myrocardial infarction and cardiogenic shock at the same time. What a massive blow he must have experienced."

The younger doctor nodded. "Three days. I never thought he would make it. I wager he had angina pectoris, too."

The senior doctor shrugged. "Without a doubt."

A short, gray haired man was waiting at the end of the hall.

"Doctor Martin?" he inquired of the approaching physicians.

The older doctor stopped. "Yes."

"I'm George Brighton, manager of the Metropolitan Life Insurance Company, Northeast District. Keith Masters is one of my assistant managers. How is he?"

"He's doing as well as can be expected, Mr. Brighton. I believe one of your people was in a day or two ago, to arrange for his hospitalization insurance."

"Yes. I sent over one of our other assistant managers. I realize it's somewhat premature to make a definite statement, but what is Mr. Masters' actual condition?"

The doctor hedged. "It's quite uncertain at this point."

Brighton smiled wryly. "Doctor, I am an attorney by training. Furthermore, in my profession as an insurance company manager, I deal with these matters extensively."

Martin raised an eyebrow. "All right, Mr. Brighton. His attack should not be fatal, but we won't have a complete evaluation of the damage to his heart until a few more tests have been made. The one thing we can guess is that the next attack will be much more severe. It could come tomorrow, or in ten years."

"Will he be able to return to work, or would you consider it a permanent disability?"

The doctor pursed his lips. "As an educated guess, I think he should be up and around in three or four months. But if he should do any kind of work except, light, part-time duties, he will be back rather quickly."

"Then we may conclude that he is permanently disabled?"

"If he were on my staff, I would order him to remain at home for a year and search for a hobby."

The insurance manager nodded. "Thank you, doctor." He left the hospital and drove directly back to his office. There he picked up the phone and dialed a number taken from an information card.

A woman's voice answered.

"Hello, Gloria. This is George Brighton."

"Why, hello, Mr. Brighton. This is quite unexpected."

Brighton did not hesitate. "Gloria, Keith is ill."

There was a moment of silence. "Oh?"

"It's quite serious. A heart attack. He's in City Hospital."

There was a longer period of silence, then a sigh. "Why don't you call Keith's whore, Mr. Brighton? I'm no longer related to him. I even have a divorce certificate to prove it."

"Take it easy, Gloria. You know they broke up five years ago. I thought perhaps that Bert should know."

The woman's voice was suddenly angry. "Look, Keith walked out on us seven years ago. Bert was only eleven years old then, and he's grown up fully convinced that his father is nothing better than a worthless bastard. Furthermore, I'm remarried, and my husband and Bert are great friends. Frankly, we don't care if we ever see Keith Masters again." She hung up.

A choir was singing Silent Night on the television set when a knock came at the door. "Come in," called Masters.

The door opened and George Brighton entered. He adjusted his eyes to the dimness of the room. "Hello, Keith. I was just driving by and thought I'd drop in to wish you a Merry Christmas."

Masters grinned. "I bet you were just driving by, George. How far out of the way was it? A couple of miles?"

Brighton grinned back. He took a seat facing Masters, huddled in his chair with a shawl around his shoulders. "You've put on some weight," he observed.

"I'm up to one hundred and thirty now. Still twenty pounds under."

"Well, you don't look too bad for a guy on full pension. How are you making out?"

"I should have gotten sick sooner. It's the first time I ever caught up with my bills." He studied the gray haired man. "George, did you call Gloria when I became ill?"

Brighton nodded. "She was still pretty angry."

Masters pursed his lips, his face still slate looking. "Just like her. She'll carry the grudge right to the grave, fighting like a son-of-a-bitch to drag everyone else along. How about Bert?"

"She said he didn't want to see you. Bert didn't say it. She did."

"Then you can bet your bottom dollar that it's true. He was a fine little fellow until she got on his ear. I hope he never realizes what kind of a mother he has. Hating his father is bad enough."

"What ever happened between you two? You and Gloria were a real handsome couple."

Masters leaned back into his chair. "I honestly don't know, George. Gloria is a damned good looking woman, and I thought we had it made. Then, all of a sudden, about two or three years after Bert was born, she changed. At first I thought it was the mother versus father grab for the kid's affection, but it wasn't that. Right off the bat she started acting as if she was the greatest piece of ass in the world, like she could lay back and eat an apple while you were knocking it off, and that you should rave about it for a week afterwards. Then the great withdrawal act, the suffering heroine putting up with all the crap in the world and keeping a stiff upper lip even though she had a bastard for a husband." He shook his head. "I couldn't figure it out. I thought maybe I wasn't cutting the mustard in bed. Half the troubles of the world start there. But when this thing came up, I was hitting on all eight cylinders and she was jumping around and yelling like it was the greatest thing she ever knew."

He drew the shawl tighter around his shoulders. "Maybe it was because I wasn't earning all the money in the world. Gloria considered herself a pretty high-class article."

Brighton took out a pack of cigarettes, then self-consciously shoved it back into a pocket.

"Go ahead, smoke," said Masters. "I get the willies as bad whether you smoke or not."

Brighton lit one up. "I was never able to understand," he said, blowing smoke away from Masters, "why you were content to stay on a debit for so many years before I could persuade you to take an assistant manager's job."

Masters picked up a piece of hard rock candy and popped it into his mouth. "Maybe not all of us are big, determined men. I just never had the gumption to do anything but ride around and collect the three bucks each month. I was content. The only reason I took the assistancy was to get a few more dollars. I'll tell you straight, George, there were a couple of hundred times I wanted to shove it right back. It was worse than digging ditches."

Brighton stood up. "Well, I've got to be going. Glad to see you're back to normal. How about coming in and having lunch with me when you're able to?"

Once the door closed behind the gray-haired man, Masters rose from the chair, switched off the group still singing Christmas carols, drew back the covers on the sofa, and lay down.

He folded his hands behind his head and thought back. I'm forty-five-years-old now. At age zero, I am a red ball of meat in a skinny woman's belly. The fellow that put me there was a railroad conductor. He had also started my brother two years before. Then he walked smack in front of a beer delivery truck - and exit a father. At five years old, I have a step-father, a barber. It wasn't too bad until he blew the claim money my mother got from the beer company, then he started cutting hair elsewhere. At age ten, my brother, Ed, and I are out peddling papers on the streets of windy Chicago, and my mother is working in a shirt factory. At age fifteen, I screw - what the hell was her name? Margot? Margaret? Well, it doesn't make much difference, except that I got scared afterwards thinking I might have caught the clap, so I put alcohol on my pecker. It hurt worse than the clap - I think. At twenty, I have already buried my mother, who is dead from a crummy pair of lungs. The skinny woman. I guess that's what saints must have looked like, for she certainly was one. At twenty-five, I have killed maybe fifteen or twenty men, all legally, and they even gave me medals for it. I also received the medal they awarded posthumously to my brother, Ed, who was scattered somewhere over the French countryside. At thirty, it is Gloria, and my son, Bert. At thirty-five, I have been recalled by the army for duty in Korea, am back out of the service, and Gloria has her tail up in the air. At forty, it is...

"Keith," said Cathy. "I don't see any reason why we can't get married."

"For Christ's sake," he replied, putting down the newspaper. "Are we going to go all over that again? I'm paying every dime I earn for alimony to Gloria. I haven't bought a goddamn shirt in two years. How the hell can we get married?"

"It doesn't make any difference. We're getting along now, aren't we? If we can get along now, we can get along the same if we're married."

He eyed her with irritation. "Do you know something? You're probably the best piece of ass in Chicago and most certainly the dumbest. I don't know how the fuck I've put up with you for two years." He mimicked her. "If we can get along now we can get along the same as now." He threw the newspaper to the floor. "Can't you get it through your thick, Polack skull that I just got rid of one wife and I don't want another."

Her lips trembled. "You don't love me," she wailed.

He jumped to his feet, his face flushed with rage. "No!" he shouted. "I don't love you. You're just an orgasm, a crying, nagging, smothering nobody who isn't worth a shit ten minutes out of bed." He stamped out of the apartment.

When he returned, hours later, reeling from too much beer, she was gone - bag and baggage.

Masters turned over onto his side. Now forty-five - and a half-dead man. God Almighty, what is wrong with me? Why can't I find just a little of the peace I've searched for all my life? It's as if a rot has been placed inside me, that I have been condemned to unhappiness.

And then, for the first time in twenty years, he forced himself to admit it. Yes, I knew Schneider was going to raise his rifle and shoot that Jap sergeant. I knew it the moment he came up and aimed and fired. I could have stopped it. I could have said, "Do not fire." I could have even pushed up his weapon. But I didn't. Because I wanted him to shoot!

God Almighty! I've murdered a man!

CHAPTER 2

In the morning, Masters made his way slowly down the three flights of stairs to the basement and unlocked the small, storage room provided for each tenant of the old, apartment house. Inside were two battered footlockers, a dust covered Valapack, and a Samsonite suitcase. He sat on a footlocker for a few minutes to rest, then kneeled and opened one. Among the folders of army orders, certificates, Veterans Administration letters regarding his pension for wounds, and personal papers, he found the wallet and the thousand-stitch belt.

Back in his one-roomed apartment, he opened the wallet. It was mildewed, cracked, and heavy with the odor of the sands, cliffs and volcano ash. The small amount of Japanese money was gone. Bert had swiped it when he was six or seven years old to show round the neighborhood. It had then disappeared casually, as if it had been placed in a clothes drawer and had fallen to the floor while the clothing was taken out, then carelessly laid on top of the bureau to be swept up during a periodic housecleaning.

Directly in the center of the wallet and its contents was a jagged hole, bored out by one of his submachine bullets on its way through the pocket of the Japanese sergeant's shirt before thundering into his chest. Master lifted the leather flap and took out a picture and a small, white name card.

The picture and the card were stuck together. He sat in a chair next to the single lamp in the room and peered closely at the photo. It was of a short, slim man of twenty-two or so, seated on a bench in a photo studio and wearing a khaki uniform and visored cap. Master strained to see if he had stripes of rank on his collar or sleeves, but the picture was too distorted by the passage of time. On his lap was a child. It would have to be a boy, for he wore a little visored cap similar to that of the soldier. The features of the man and child were blurred. He tried to guess the boy's age. Perhaps six months old.

Standing slightly behind and to one side of the soldier was his wife, a slender woman, straight as a reed, dressed in a kimono, her hair piled high on her head and perfectly arranged. He could not see her face, for the bullet had torn squarely through it. In her left arm she held another child, about two years old, who was likewise dressed in a kimono with an obi peeking out from the side. The girl's face was the clearest. It was long, serious, containing large, expressive eyes and a pixie-type snub nose.

Masters sat fascinated by the picture, putting it down with great reluctance at noon to eat a frugal lunch and to take a nap. When he awoke, he continued studying it until suppertime, then, when he had eaten; he put on a pot of water to boil and held the photo and card over the steam. Patiently, he moved his hand to and fro until he had them unstuck, giving a sigh of relief to see them come apart without damage.

The name card bore a line of Japanese characters running from top to bottom. The bullet had entered a bit off center and touched one of the characters, but they were all readily identifiable.

He placed the card and photo on the lamp stand to dry, then switched on the television. Frequently, during the evening, he turned off the television set and picked them up, staring as intently as before.

The following morning, he bundled up warmly and descended the staircase to a store at a corner. There he looked up a telephone number, then entered a booth and dialed.

A woman's voice answered. "Berlitz Language School, good morning."

"Do you have courses in Japanese?" asked Masters.

"Of course, sir. Three times weekly, on Mondays, Wednesdays and Fridays, at seven p.m."

He hesitated. "How much are they?"

"One moment, please." A short time later she was back. "In a group course, it is seventy-two dollars for twelve weeks."

"Thank you."

That evening, Masters registered at the school, disappointed to learn that new classes would not begin until after the first of the year.

"Could I speak with the instructor for a few minutes, please?" he asked the registration clerk.

The clerk glanced at her watch. "I don't think he's started his classes yet." She directed him to the proper room.

The instructor was a stout, middle-aged Japanese. Masters handed him the card.

"Could you please tell me what is written here?"

"It's a name. Ito Tanaka."

"Does it have any meaning?"

The Japanese shook his head. "No, it's just a name. Quite often a woman carries a name with a meaning, such as a flower or an incident, but it's rare for a man. It's a common name, though, this Ito Tanaka. Probably a farmer or a villager."

Masters walked home slowly, muttering, "Ito Tanaka. Ito Tanaka."

The next morning, he made his way to his former insurance office. George Brighton was in his office checking over delinquent accounts.

"For Pete's sake, Keith," he said, getting up to help Masters doff his overcoat. He placed it on a rack near the door. "What are you doing out in this weather? Don't you know it's freezing outside?"

Masters took the seat offered by Brighton and smiled. "Of all the things I'm not afraid of, it's catching cold. George, I want to borrow on my policies."

"All right, Keith." He rang for a clerk and told her to fill out the forms. "Do you want the money right away?"

"No, let it come through normally." He hesitated. "I'm going to Japan this summer."

"Japan! Are you out of your mind?"

Masters leaned over the desk. "George, you're one of the most understanding people I know." He gnawed gently at his lip for a few moments, concentrating on how he should express himself. "A couple of nights ago, right after you left, I started thinking about myself. I guess when you've faced death as closely as I did last summer, you begin to ask yourself some questions."

Brighton interrupted. "You've faced death long before last summer. What about the War, and Korea?"

"That's different. I was a husky kid then. In battle you know one thing - if you don't get the big one that day, you're still young and healthy and can fight like a son-of-a-bitch the next day. Since last summer, I learned that I can't fight anymore. All I can do is delay the big one."

"Okay, Keith. You've got something on your mind. Let's have it."

Masters sighed and chewed his lip harder. "A couple of nights ago I realized that I had murdered a man."

Brighton eyes opened wide in surprise for the merest moment, then he got up, strode to the far end of the office and shut the door, which was slightly ajar. He took his seat, his expression guarded. "Keith," he said softly. "Do you know what you're saying?"

Masters raised his hand. "Relax, George. The killing was considered legal. In fact, they gave medals for it."

Relief spread over Brighton's face. "You mean the war, don't you?"

"Yes. I was responsible for the murder of a man." The manager sat quietly, eyeing him. "I allowed one of my sergeants to shoot this Jap. I could have stopped it, but I didn't. I guess I've always known I was responsible for his death, but I was unable to admit it to myself until a couple of nights ago."

"Was he a soldier - this Japanese?"

"Yes."

"Was he armed?"

"Yes."

"Had he surrendered?"

"No, but he was severely wounded. He wasn't able to fight anymore."

"Did you order this sergeant to shoot him?"

"No." Masters paused, then sighed. "But I wanted him to."

Brighton leaned back, lit a cigarette while he digested what Masters had said, then blew smoke towards the ceiling. "Keith, I was with the Judge Advocate during the war. Your case occurred so many times that you couldn't count them. There isn't a court in the world which would find against you - or your sergeant. You are in the midst of a firefight and you put a bullet into an enemy. An enemy, Keith. Get that word fixed in your mind. The enemy is sworn to kill you, any way he can. Anyhow, after you put a bullet into this...enemy, you take out insurance by putting another bullet into him. Whether he's kicking or not, you shoot him good. I think that's being a smart soldier, not a murderer."

"And if he had surrendered?"

"That's different."

"And you conclude that a wounded man, unable to lift a finger, is not the same? Maybe he wanted to surrender, but didn't have the strength or time to turn his head and say so."

"That's known as real tough titty, Keith, and if you've heard one bullet fly by your head, you know it's the truth." Brighton hesitated. "Look, I'm not a psychoanalyst, and you're not the kind of person who needs to be told that your heart attack has released all sorts of fantasies. I assume that you firmly believe what you are saying, and that it had lain dormant - how long?"

"Twenty years."

"Okay, twenty years. Furthermore, because it happened twenty years ago doesn't mitigate it nor make it any the less important. I also see that even though you didn't pull the trigger yourself, you feel a moral guilt. But moral guilt, or even actual guilt, is something we all have inside us in some form or another, and we have to live with it. Look at Hank Wasinski. Every time he lays with his wife and uses a rubber he believes he is committing a mortal sin. It preys on his mind, but it must be lived with."

"But he hasn't murdered."

"That's not the way Hank sees it. But let's get one point straight right now. You haven't murdered anyone. I don't speak of it in just a legal sense, because legally you have complied with all the rules of warfare, even though your enemy, and again, I repeat, your enemy, did not believe in nor abide by the Geneva Convention Rules of Warfare. Morally, you had two alternatives, to fight for his life, if you felt disposed to, or to take it, and taking it was the result of every bit of training you ever had in the army." Brighton shook his head. "Keith, you cannot castigate yourself for this incident."

Masters sat quietly, reflecting. "Thanks, George, you've explained yourself well and I understand what you have said. But I still think differently, and I am not trying to build up a case because I have nothing better to do or to make a mountain out of a molehill. Look." He leaned forward again, trying desperately to explain himself. "You find a man lying on the ground, bleeding from a wound which requires only a slight pressure on the artery to stop it. He can be a complete stranger, or a guy whose guts you hate. You walk away and let him bleed to death. Are you guilty?"

Brighton met Masters' eyes levelly. "You are not guilty of murder," he said softly. Under Masters continuing stare, he finally looked down at his desk. There was a long silence. "What do you expect to accomplish in Japan, Keith?" he asked.

"I don't know, George, I don't know. Maybe seek atonement for my sin. I must do something besides sit here and think of it." He rose and held out his hand. "So long, George."

Brighton stood up. "Do what you must, Keith. But keep in touch."

The old, battered cargo ship came alongside the dock in Yokohama. Masters stood at the rail to watch the Japanese stevedores, garbed in cotton shorts and sleeveless shirts, with red sweat-bands on their foreheads, swarm along the piers loading and unloading ships. The brisk, salt tanged air caught up the scent of fish and frying oils mingled with the harsh odors of radish and peppers and cabbage. The small, heavily muscled workers were an orderly mass, wheeling forklifts and swinging cranes.

The July weather was bright, invigorating, and the slow trip across the Pacific had worked wonders for the lonely man with the defective heart.

His eyes turned to the southeast, to the Hommokumisaki, the promontory known as Treaty Point. For a moment his thoughts went back to his rest leave from Korea and to the Japanese girl whose name he could never pronounce, whom he had nicknamed 'Betty Grable'. She had taken him sightseeing at the promontory, and had said, "Here's where it all started, the flow of foreigners which has never stopped." They had sat there looking out over the bay, then had decided that going back to their hotel in Tokyo would take too much time, so they had rushed to one nearby to do what Masters had come to Japan to do.

He glanced towards the north, unable to see but sensing the movement of the unbelievably crowded Tokyo, remembering the long strolls through the teeming streets where he felt like a giant among the short, slim, beautiful Orientals.

His clearance through immigration and customs took but a few minutes, and he was amused at the results obtained by speaking his limited Japanese, for there was always a bow and a smile. The three months at the Berlitz school were not completely wasted.

He was directed to a bus and sat next to a heavy-browed Japanese, who kept his eyes glued to a newspaper while the vehicle raced recklessly through the narrow streets of Yokohama and into the maelstrom of the Shitamachi, or downtown Tokyo. Masters had to agree that adverting one's eyes was the only defense against the terror of driving in Tokyo.

He found a small, inexpensive hotel near the terminal. The room was just wide enough to stretch his arms, but it was clean and orderly. It did not have a bathroom. The community toilet and bath were down the hallway.

His first call was at the American Embassy, where he learned that the agency which handled veterans' matters was the Gunjin Kazoku Enjo Kyokai, The Association for the Protection of Families of Soldiers. As it was now too late to visit, he walked the streets to see the changes which fourteen years had wrought. It was like being in Chicago or New York or Philadelphia - if one could read the Japanese characters over the stores.

He stopped abruptly at the first pachinko stand, a sparkle coming to his eyes as he brought twenty-five small, steel balls, and put them one by one into the machine, pulling the trigger and watching them shoot up, then work their way downward through the scores of nails to the various slots at the bottom. He hit the winning slots a number of times, took a handful of the balls back to the counter, and received three bars of candy in exchange.

He strolled by the Emperor's Palace, stopping to watch the fat, golden carp swim lazily in the moat and wonder how many generations of fish had come and gone since he had last gazed into the same moat. In a simple restaurant in the Ginza section, he ordered boiled fish and vegetables which he had seen served to another customer. He pointed it out to the waitress, for he did not know how to ask for it in Japanese.

The next morning, he found the Association for Protection of the Families of Soldiers, and was taken in tow by a middle-aged man who spoke English.

"Ito Tanaka? Iwo Jima? Please wait here." In half an hour, he returned with a dossier. "Yes, we have him. He was a sergeant in an engineer battalion at Iwo Jima." He pronounced battalion as "battarian", since most Japanese were unable to use the letter 'l'. His face saddened. "We have absolutely no information as to what happened to most of the twenty-two thousand people on the island. With the exception of a handful who surrendered, we have listed all others as having been killed in action."

"We had several thousand casualties, too," said Masters, remembering quite clearly saying goodbye at the graves of many of his men and fellow officers before leaving the island.

It caught the man short. "Yes, of course," he mumbled.

"Tanaka's family? What about them?"

The man scanned the dossier again. "As of nineteen-fifty, his wife and two children were residing near Kawaba, a small village about seventy-five miles northwest of here. That was sixteen years ago. I would assume that they are still there."

"Why would you assume that?"

"The Nipponese peasant remains with the land, especially a widow with two small children."

"How can I find out for certain?"

"The National Police would be able to assist you."

The National Police were indeed helpful. Within minutes, a sergeant, eyeing Masters curiously, wrote out a name and address on a slip of paper.

"Mrs. Tanaka now resides in Tokyo," he said. "Is it possible to explain why you are looking for her?"

"It's a personal matter." Masters observed a gleam of amusement flicker across the sergeant's eyes. "Does something amuse you, buster?" he growled.

The gleam instantly disappeared. "Of course not," he replied politely, handing over the slip of paper. On it was written, 'Kimiko Tanaka' and an address.

Outside the police headquarters, Masters flagged down a cab and showed the slip of paper to the driver. "Yamanote," said the driver as Masters stepped inside, and promptly took off with a breathtaking dash of speed.

Masters found the word in his information book with an explanation that it was the finest residential section of Tokyo.

The taxi drove west into the suburbs and drew up in front of a large, magnificently designed one-story house of polished, white stone, its roof of glistening red tiles rising at the eaves in a classical Japanese arch. A fastidiously tended garden surrounded the house, and was in turn enclosed by a high, bamboo fence. Masters looked with dismay at the driver.

"Is this the right house?" he asked.

The driver nodded. "Yes, Mister. Same address as on paper."

"You'd better wait." He climbed out, opened the gate, walked up the flag-stone pathway to the front door and knocked. A small, wizened woman came to the door. "Mrs. Tanaka?" he asked.

The old woman, a number of teeth missing, bowed and answered.

"What?" asked Masters, not understanding her.

She spoke again.

Masters shook his head. "Is Mrs. Tanaka here?" he asked once more.

The taxi driver, observing the situation, came up and talked to the woman. He turned to Masters. "Mrs. Tanaka," he explained, "lives here. Not home before seven o'clock tonight. Works at store downtown."

"Can you get the address of the store?"

The driver spoke briefly to the servant. "Have address. You want to go there?"

"Yes."

The driver turned his vehicle and drove to the Ginza sector of downtown Tokyo, where he drew up in front of a large, fashionable shop. Masters paid him off, then glanced through the windows as he slowly strolled by. It was an exclusive women's boutique, selling lingerie, dresses, sweaters and night wear. Six or seven smartly dressed saleswomen were waiting on customers. Masters walked on a couple of blocks, took a coffee, then returned. It was still busy inside. His eyes passed over the women inside, hoping to pick out the one he was seeking. Two of them were about her age.

He waited for a lull in the business, then entered. A young woman came up at once. "May I help you, please?" she asked in Japanese.

"I am looking for Mrs. Tanaka."

"One moment, please." The salesgirl knocked at a door at the rear of the store and went inside. A short while later, a woman came out.

Masters studied her closely as she approached. She was a small woman, about five feet tall, slender, with black hair drawn tight into a bun at the back of her head in the old-fashioned manner. He saw immediately that she had had eye operations to reduce the slant, and that her cheeks and lips were slightly touched by cosmetics.

She was an elegant woman, typically Japanese, well formed, erect, walking with a graceful air. He guessed her age to be forty.

"I am Mrs. Tanaka," she said, keeping her eyes from looking directly at him, another old custom.

"My name is Keith Masters," he started in Japanese.

"Would you prefer to speak English?" she asked, with only a faint accent.

"Yes, very much so," he replied, relieved. He glanced round. "Could we speak privately?"

"Of course. Please." She led the way to the office in the rear. It was tastefully furnished, a polished walnut desk, two slim straight-backed chairs, a cushioned sofa, and thick wall to wall carpeting. Fresh flowers were on the desk, carefully arranged in a hand-painted vase. She motioned courteously for him to be seated while she remained standing.

He drew in a deep breath as he reached into an inner pocket of his jacket. "Do you recognize this?" he asked, handing her the photo.

She took it with a bow of her head and glanced at it. Suddenly, her eyes widened and her lips parted. The color flew from her face. A slender hand darted to her mouth to stifle the cry welling up. Her black, intense eyes flashed towards Masters, eyes filled with a groping hope mingled with the terror of final judgment.

"Where is he?" she finally whispered hoarsely.

"He is dead," said Master bluntly. "Sit down, Mrs. Tanaka." Her eyes had closed and her hands had covered her face. She stood rigid, silently weeping, then began to rock with grief. "Do you want some water?" he asked. She shook her head.

He rose and walked to the window behind the desk. It faced a cobblestone alley where half-a-dozen boys were playing baseball with a small wooden bat and a rubber ball. He deliberately looked away until she regained her composure.

"Where did you get the picture? How do you know that my husband is dead?" The two questions were whispers.

He turned. "I was on Iwo Jima. One of my men took it from the body of a Japanese sergeant. He gave it to me."

She was fighting desperately for control. "Was it definitely my husband?"

He nodded. "It was him. I will go now." He started towards the door.

She trembled as if he had struck her. "Please, please, do not go. There is so much I want to ask."

He stopped. "All right." Picking up a pencil from the desk, he wrote his name and hotel on a pad. "I am staying here. I will not leave until we speak again."

She gave a sigh of relief. "Please, Mr. Masters." She glanced quickly at her watch. "I will be leaving in an hour. Would you visit my home this evening, for dinner?"

"I'll come over afterwards. Eight o'clock."

"Do you know the address?"

"Yes. I was there earlier this afternoon. An old woman gave me the address of this store."

As he started from the room, Kimiko whispered pleadingly. "Please come, Mr. Masters."

He halted. "I'll be there." Then he went out.

At exactly eight o'clock, the taxi drew up in front of the house. Kimiko was waiting at the door, as if she had been standing there since the moment of her return. Her eyes lighted up with relief.

"Good evening, Mr. Masters," she greeted him with a bow. "Thank you for coming." She led him into the living room. It was unusually large, its walls covered by delicately colored silk cloth. Two Italian provincial sofas, matching armchairs, and hand-carved, straight-backed Louis XIV chairs of oiled cherry wood were tastefully located. To one side stood a combination television-stereo set. He was surprised, for it was totally European. So unlike his opinion of her being traditionally Japanese.

A young, stunningly beautiful girl, wearing a sheath-like dress, was seated on one of the straight-backed chairs. She stood up as they entered.

She would be about twenty-three or four, reasoned Masters.

"This is my daughter, Hiroko," said Kimiko.

The girl was taller and more rounded than her mother. They shook hands in the western fashion. "Good evening, Mr. Masters," she said easily, although it was evident that she had heard of him and knew the reason for his visit.

"Would you care for something to drink?" asked Kimiko. He could see from her deep breathing that she was controlling her nervousness only by a great effort.

"I cannot drink whisky," he replied. "May I have tea?"

"Of course. I would be most pleased." She walked quickly to the kitchen to give instructions.

Masters took a seat on the sofa across from the girl. He could hardly keep his eyes from her. The long, narrow face in the picture was still the same, the skin a flawless ivory, subtly rouged, and the almond-shaped eyes which filled her face held the same soft, black irises of her mother. Her hair was piled high on her head, held in place by a band of sparkling rhinestones.

"Mother said you know of my father." She spoke English fluently, with the merest hint of a lisp.

"Yes. I wish it could have been happy news. I'm sorry."

"You must not be. We have always been certain that he..." her voice lowered, "...was dead. But there was still the constant shred of doubt which lingered in my mother's mind and it caused her considerable sadness. Now, at least, she will be able to accept the finality of his death." She leaned forward. "Please, Mr. Masters, my mother is from the old Japanese way of life. It will be very difficult for her to ask you to speak. This is because of our custom between man and woman. Please help her."

Hiroko broke off the conversation as Kimiko led in the wrinkled servant carrying a tray. When they were served, Kimiko sat on a stiff-backed chair and folded her hands. Her eyes fastened on Masters.

"Please, Mr. Masters, would you tell us all you know about my husband."

Masters sipped the fragrant drink slowly to collect his thoughts. "I was a platoon leader on Iwo Jima," he said slowly. "We were mopping up in the hill area at the north end of the island. A group of our men had a fight with four Japanese soldiers in a cave along the beach - and killed them. A wallet and a thousand-stitch belt was taken from your husband."

"Did you see him?" whispered Kimiko.

"Yes."

"How did he die?" she whispered again, brokenly. Her jaw muscles were tight and the skin of her hands shone white with the pressure upon them.

"He died instantly. Without pain. He died fighting - as a soldier."

A small sigh escaped from Kimiko's lips. "Thank you with all my heart, Mr. Masters, for having come to tell us." She was struggling to control the tears. "Do you know where I can find the body?"

They had left the corpses to the sun and the sea crabs. Perhaps burial patrols had found them later - to fling the remains into the common burial pit with the thousands of other enemy soldiers.

"He was taken to the main Japanese cemetery and interred with his comrades. There were no means by which our forces could keep individual records, so they were buried together."

"Who killed my father?"

Masters' head lifted at the sharp question from Hiroko. Her eyes were flashing.

"Hiroko" called Kimiko, appalled that a guest, especially a man, should be spoken to in such a manner.

"That's all right, Mrs. Tanaka, she's entitled to know." He turned back to the beautiful girl and looked at her levelly. "There were many soldiers shooting at the same time, not only at your father but also at his three comrades. It would be impossible to say which one actually killed him."

"Did you shoot also?" she asked bluntly.

A dark silence fell over the room. Masters slowly placed the teacup and saucer on the table by his side and stood up.

"Yes. I shot, too," he replied quietly.

In the utter stillness, he strode to the door and let himself out, then walked slowly down the street until he found a passing taxi that took him to his hotel.

31

Back in his small room, he lay fully dressed on the bed, listening to the pounding of the tired organ he called a heart, feeling no release of relief, no sense of expiation, only a heaviness and inertia. When dawn began to steal through the single window of his room, he finally fell into a fitful slumber.

CHAPTER 3

It was almost noon when Masters descended to the narrow lobby of the hotel. To his surprise, Kimiko was waiting there, sitting stiffly erect on a chair in a corner. She rose as he came down the staircase.

"Good morning, Mr. Masters," she said. "I hope you will forgive my intrusion."

"That's all right, Mrs. Tanaka. Have you been waiting long?"

"Since eight o'clock," she answered simply, directly, and he wondered if she had ever told a lie, even a white one, in her whole life.

"I'm sorry. You should have asked the clerk to waken me."

"I did not mind waiting. Have you eaten?"

"Not yet."

"May I join you, please?"

"Of course." He guided her out into the street. It was a bright, sunny day, warm and balmy, the street crowded with workers and shoppers going to lunch or idling the time away. "There is a tea room two blocks away," he said. "Would that be okay?"

"Yes, thank you."

He studied her from the corner of his eye as she walked gracefully beside him, halfway between the short, quick step of the older Japanese women and the free swinging stride of a young girl. She seemed to be partial to suits, and wore a trim, linen skirt and jacket with a white, nylon blouse which accented the smooth, somewhat dusky lines of her throat. She was a very attractive woman and he enjoyed walking at her side.

"Won't you have trouble, taking off work all morning?" he asked.

"I am the owner of the boutique, Mr. Masters. It is one of eighteen stores in my chain." She was unable to conceal her pride, even with a great effort.

He stopped. "I hadn't thought of that. Yes, that lovely home of yours - and the office at the store. I thought perhaps you were the manager. I congratulate you, Mrs. Tanaka."

As her eyes lowered and she bowed her thanks, he could see that she was pleased with his comment.

At the restaurant she ordered a salad while he asked for a roll and tea. "Is that all you are eating?" she asked in surprise.

He answered easily. "Doctor's orders. I had a bit of a heart condition a year ago."

Her brow rose with sudden alertness. "Oh, Mr. Masters, please forgive Hiroko and me. We did not suspect. I also want to apologize for her manners last night. It was unforgivable."

He shrugged. "She had a right to ask the questions."

Kimiko shook her head vigorously. "You were a guest in our home and she embarrassed you. I am afraid that I built up the image of her father too greatly over the years and neglected to teach her self-discipline."

"Aren't you also bitter at the thought that I might have been one of the men who killed your husband?"

She sighed. "I am bitter only when I remember the waste. The years have taught me to accept the manner of his death. It was a needless, senseless war, and I cannot forgive those who permitted it to occur. But I realize that my husband, and you, were soldiers who had to obey the commands of your superiors in doing what you considered was right." She looked down at the table. "My heart is lighter knowing that he did not suffer and that he is with his companions. Twenty years of uncertainty, Mr. Masters, had brought to my mind many horrible pictures which made the loss even greater."

Their food had come, and they were eating while talking. Masters stopped chewing. "What kind of man was your husband?" he asked.

A wistful smile tugged at her lips. "He was a great man. A kind, wonderful person." Her face lit up as a thought came to her. "Do you have any plans for the weekend, Mr. Masters?"

"No. I was going to check on a return passage to the United States, but a few more days won't make any difference."

Her face registered dismay. "You will leave soon? Oh no."

"It's not I must leave, Mrs. Tanaka." He shrugged again. "There is just nothing here to keep me." He paused as the thought struck. "In fact, there is nothing on the other end either."

"There is no family, Mr. Masters?"

He sipped the remainder of his tea, then shook his head.

Kimiko's eyes lowered, like a high school girl about to ask a boy for a date. "Would you like to visit the area where my husband and I were raised?"

He was about to say "not really", but "yes" slipped out.

"Thank you. Tomorrow is Saturday. Would it be convenient to leave at noon?"

"That's all right with me."

They rose from the table, he paid the bill and guided her back to the street. She turned and bowed. "Thank you for lunch, Mr. Masters." Then bowing again, as if she was shaking his hand, she disappeared in the throng passing by.

At noon the following day, Kimiko arrived at the hotel driving a new, expensive Datsun sedan. Masters eyed the wild Tokyo traffic as he climbed apprehensively into the car.

"Good morning," she said, moving smoothly into the streaming madhouse. She drove well, not challenging the wildness of the other drivers, and not being bluffed either, but fitting into the pattern and the flow calmly and without effort.

Soon they were in the countryside, where Kimiko pointed out the points of interest, as if she was a guide for a special tour, and later stopped the car for lunch at an isolated hotel in the rolling hills. It had a small restaurant, containing less than a dozen tables, but since they had arrived after the rush hour, they were seated at once.

"They have a marvelous fish soup," she explained. "It will be good for you." Masters raised a brow, and she suddenly blushed, then quickly ordered to cover her confusion.

The soup was excellent, and so was the tea which they drank seated by a window that overlooked a grove of poplars and listened to the soft patter of conversation of the few other diners who had also come in late. They did not talk much, he and Kimiko, as if now was the time for silence, and it make him comfortable to realize that she knew it as well as he.

He did not say anything either when the bill came. He could have eaten for two days in Tokyo for the same amount. The fact must have registered on his face, for Kimiko opened her mouth to say something, then closed it, as though she suddenly understood why he was staying at such a small, inexpensive hotel.

It was past mid-afternoon when she turned off the main road onto a narrow lane that was little more than a dirt path. The countryside was not a rich land, that Masters could see. It was hilly terrain, rocky, which tolerated only small patches of ground to be farmed. It was evident that the people had striven for countless years to conquer the barren, unfriendly hills by terracing the sides with barriers of stone and hand-carrying earth up the slopes to lay over the hard, rock base.

The danger to their livelihood was even more obvious in that fierce storms could easily wash away the stone barriers and carry down the soil the farmers had so laboriously built up.

She stopped the car at the base of a jagged hill. About sixty or seventy feet up, a man working in a garden stood up and waved. He was a veritable ancient, bent and wrinkled, and his greeting brought forth from a hut situated to one side an old woman, equally bent and wrinkled. Kimiko lifted out a weekend bag, caught up Masters' shaving kit, and locked the car doors.

"I'll carry those," he said, as she started up the dirt path to the hut.

"Please," she said, smiling. "You are now in ancient Japan, Mr. Masters. It is the custom for the women to carry the parcels."

He eyed the petite, healthy woman in the light blue suit, wearing fine, Italian slippers on her feet, admiring the ripple of smooth muscles in the calves of her legs as she stepped lightly up the hill.

She's a helleva good-looking forty, he thought. Then he began to follow her up the path.

On a small landing in front of the hut, she bowed low to the old man, and when Masters finally came up, huffing and puffing, she introduced him to her father, Mr. Ishkawa. He was about seventy years old, neatly dressed in blue work clothes, with a thin beard and merry, black eyes.

Masters bowed. "Hajume-mashinte," he said, in the formal manner of greeting.

Kimiko presented him to her mother, as old as her husband and with the same twinkle in her eyes, who unabashedly appraised him like she would a chicken in the market place.

"You are the first American they have ever met," explained Kimiko.

The hut consisted of two tiny rooms with a shed at the rear, handsomely wallpapered and well furnished. Masters guessed that Kimiko had fixed up the place for her parents, and when he wondered why they chose to live the unsophisticated life of the hills when she possessed the means to provide a more comfortable existence, he remembered what the man at the Association for the Protection of Families of Soldiers had said - that the farmer remained with his soil.

One room was the traditional living-dining room, containing a kotatsu in the center. This was a wood-lined hollow in the floor, three feet square and eighteen inches deep, with a table rising about a foot above it.

He nearly burst out laughing when he thought back almost fifteen years to the time an artillery major and he had taken off for a weekend while attending an air-ground course at Camp Drake just outside of Tokyo. They had visited a neighboring village for the express purpose of tracking down a somewhat famous whorehouse that boasted of extraordinary beautiful partners and unusually low prices, and while the owner was sending out for the girls who lived nearby, the major had sat at the kotatsu and opened a bottle of scotch. His girl had arrived soon after, a splendid looking whore, with the information that Masters' woman would be along a bit later.

They had played strip poker to while away the time, and soon the major was so cock-eyed drunk that he was barely able to read the cards. Masters had really stacked them after that. Within a short time, the major was almost naked and pulling up the blanket being used as a tablecloth around his waist to keep from chattering from the cold. The girl, who did not know what in the devil the game was all about, was taking off her clothes and laying them on the pile building up beside Masters. She struggled to the end to keep her breasts from being exposed, even to the point of giving up her panties first, and finally they were bared, half-mooned, dusky melons with large, proud paps which tightened from the cold, and she had called the owner, who slipped a small, charcoal burning hibachi under the kotatsu to keep them warm.

It was fortunate that Masters' whore had finally come, for the major was not so drunk that he could not see the glint in Masters' eyes as he stared at the naked girl seated next to him...

Kimiko's mother served tea and sweet, coconut cakes, then sat down and chattered away at her daughter. But Kimiko listened with only one ear, for her attention was principally focused on Masters and her father struggling courteously to talk to each other.

As soon as it was politely possible, she led Masters outside and they sat on a bench overlooking the small plot of land her father had been working.

"Over there," she pointed to a hill a couple of miles away, "is the home of Ito, my husband." She rested her head against the wall of the hut and lifted her face towards the dying sun, closing her eyes to reminisce.

She remained silent as though caught up by swells of memory which overwhelmed her, reaching far into each corner of her brain and focusing an intense light on the pictures that years could never dim, pictures which had been taken out countless times to be burned deep into memory cells, so that slipping from mind to awareness was an automatic, effortless action. Finally, her eyes opened.

"My parents had seven children, Mr. Masters. I was next to the youngest. This piece of land," she motioned at the garden, perhaps twenty-five by fifteen feet, "was all they had. Underneath it is rock, and we searched every day for earth to build it up. We were very poor. Three of my brothers and sisters died when they were quite young, another brother was lost at sea in the navy, and a sister was killed during an airplane bombing at Osaka. The only one left is a sister who lives in Sendai."

Masters nodded. "I can see that life here must have been a hard one. But it's difficult for me to picture you as having been a country girl."

"It was Ito who was responsible, although he came from a family which was even more impoverished than ours. There were eleven children, of whom two died in infancy. Education was an absolute luxury. About five miles down the road is a small schoolhouse where most of the children would attend until they were twelve or thirteen years old, then they would seek work on a large farm or in the villages. Work was hard to find, so most of them helped their parents in the garden."

Her lips parted in a wistful smile. "I have heard many Americans comment on how beautifully our fields were tended. There were always so many children to help that a weed could not exist in this land.

"Ito was three years older than me, and we left school about the same time. He was thirteen years old then. As he was the oldest son, he labored very hard in the fields."

Her eyes closed again and her voice lowered. "I was fourteen years old when he told me I would be his wife. I was very happy, and in the evenings when work was ended he would eat quickly and come for me so we could sit up there," she pointed, eyes still closed, to a ledge about thirty feet up, "and talk of what we wanted from life.

"There was never any money, so Ito searched until he found a farmer who had books. In a land of hard-working people, I never saw a boy work so long and so hard as he did - to get those books. During the first few hours we were able to meet each week, he insisted that we study together."

Her eyes opened. "I do not know how he did it, but before he was nineteen years old he passed a test for draftsmanship and was offered a post in Kyoto as a junior draftsman."

She turned to him. "In your country it is not unusual for a poor boy to advance, so this story must seem rather trite."

"I was poor when I was a kid, too. The whole world was poor."

Kimiko was jolted. "Forgive me, Mr. Masters, if I offended you in any way."

"You didn't offend me. But go ahead - continue."

It took her a moment to recollect herself. "Well," she went on, "to us, it was like finding gold on the street. We were married immediately, then went, halfway on foot, to Kyoto. It took eight days to get there, and until Ito drew his first pay, we slept in parks and alleys, and soon afterwards I found work in a factory. In a few months we were enormously rich." She fought off a tear. "When I look back, we had saved perhaps the sum we spent for our lunch on the way here."

Masters looked up, realizing that she had understood his reaction at the restaurant.

"But to us," she continued, "it was everything in the world. Ito, however, would not permit us to save any more. He insisted that we spend it for night school. We could have had a nice room with a kitchen, but no - we lived in a hovel as large as the shed there and spent the money to learn.

"Then Hiroko was born, but I kept on working and we were very, very happy. Ito was promoted twice, becoming the foreman of his section, and we rented two beautiful rooms with a kitchen - and even sent home small sums to our parents. But always we had to go to school. Once I said it cost too much to have a woman watch over Hiroko while I was at school, and Ito became angry - so I never said it again.

"Then Ichiro was born…" Her voice trailed off.

"Your son?" prompted Masters.

Kimiko rose and almost ran through the garden to an outcrop of rock, pressing her face against it. Masters stood up, surprised, then followed her. He saw that she was trembling. He placed a hand on her arm.

"What is it, Mrs. Tanaka? Are you ill?"

She shook her head, and Masters moved to one side to see her face. She turned it from him, but not before he saw the tears streaming down her cheeks.

Soon she controlled herself with a great effort, and reached into a pocket to take out a handkerchief to wipe her eyes. "It is nothing," she said, and from the firmness of her voice he knew that the conversation was ended. She suddenly observed that it was getting dark. "Come, it is time to eat now."

In honor of the American guest, her mother had prepared a large bowl of sukiyaki, vegetables fried with onions and lightly seasoned with sugar, soya sauce, and a few drops of saki. It was kept warm by a candle burning underneath, and next to the bowl was a platter of thin slices of raw meat, each the size of a half dollar.

Kimiko served Masters, placing bits of meat on top of the vegetable mixture to heat as they ate, and putting only small portions onto his plate so that the meat was always warm and not overcooked.

"My father," said Kimiko, when Masters finally leaned back with a satisfied sigh, "asks why you have come to Japan."

Masters answered Mr. Ishkawa himself. "To visit. I had been here in nineteen-fifty-two during the Korean action, and liked it."

"Are you a soldier?" asked the old man.

"Not any longer. I was in the life insurance business, but am now on a physical disability pension." Kimiko had to help him explain it, especially what a physical disability pension was.

"I hope your heart will not be affected by the climb," said Kimiko apprehensively.

"Frankly," replied Masters, smothering another groan from having overeaten, "I haven't felt as good in years."

"I am glad." She glanced at him and asked casually, "Did you visit Tokyo when you were on leave in Japan?"

"Yes, I attended two army courses at Camp Drake." He grinned. "After the Korean hills, coming to Japan was like entering a new world."

The old people were fidgeting, and Kimiko laughed. "Go," she said. They politely excused themselves, hastened to the other room, and in a few minutes Masters heard the sounds of a television set. "Imagine that," exclaimed Kimiko, still chuckling. "Television in the countryside. My parents are still overwhelmed by it. They had never seen a motion picture in their lives until now."

She arranged cushions in a corner for Masters to sit on, opened the window to let in the cool, night air, then sat facing him.

"Do you mind if I ask more questions about my husband, Mr. Masters?"

"No, but call me Keith."

"Thank you. I am Kimiko."

"I know. It's a lovely name."

She paused to study him, then leaned forward. "You said that you saw my husband when he died. How did he look? Was he tired or thin?" Her face was exceedingly sad.

Masters thought back through the years which spanned half a lifetime. "He did not appear thin or ill," he finally replied.

"When did he die?"

"I'm not sure of the exact date." He rubbed his jaw, reflecting. "It was before Okinawa was invaded - that was the first of April. I was transferred there soon after. I guess it was somewhere between the fifteenth and the thirtieth of March."

"What time of day?"

"In the afternoon, about four o'clock."

She hesitated. "Where was he shot?"

"In the heart," he said, deciding to lie. "Look, Kimiko, your husband and his comrades tried to fight back like good soldiers, but it was over in an instant."

Her head drooped and she sat silently. After a while he heard her whisper. "Do you still have the good luck belt?"

"Yes."

"May I have it, please? I made it for him."

"Yes. It's at the hotel."

Kimiko broke off the conversation as the old man and woman reentered the room. They drank tea together, then went outside to sit on the long bench in the moonlight and talk of Vietnam and Germany and Castro and China...and Masters had to chuckle at these old peasants, who know only labor all their lives, who could not read or write, but who could ask if he thought Nixon would be the Republican choice for president in 1968.

When her parents had gone to sleep in the rear room, Kimiko arranged two mats and bedding on opposite sides of the living-dining room, and waited outside while Masters disrobed and slid under the quilt. Then, in the darkened room, she changed into pajamas and lay down on her mat.

An hour passed and Masters, halfway to sleep, suddenly realized that she was sitting next to him, motionless, looking at his face in the thin light of the moon. His eyes opened fully and he raised his head from the round neck-rest.

"Yes?" he asked quietly.

She leaned down towards him. "Please, Keith," she whispered. "Did he die peacefully?"

Masters' loins suddenly grew warm, but he forced himself to answer softly. "He died peacefully, Kimiko," he replied.

"Thank you, thank you very much for having come." Then taking his hand, she pressed it, and silently padded back to her mat.

The following afternoon they started back to Tokyo. When they reached the main road, Masters turned towards her.

"Kimiko, what's the trouble with your son, Ichiro?"

Her hands tightened on the wheel. "There is a tea room a bit further on. I will tell you of him there."

When they were seated and served, she looked down at the table. Her face was white and drawn. "My son is in prison. He has killed a man. He had been sentenced to death, and our last appeal has been rejected."

"What!" exploded Masters, nearly rising from his chair.

She turned her head away to hide the tears. "It has been a nightmare. He is so much like his father, good and intelligent." She sighed. "I think it has all been my fault, speaking so often of his father. A few years ago he began to hate the Americans, and when one thing led to another, he joined the Communist Party. About a year and a half ago, a number of them assassinated a labor leader. Ichiro was one of the group. All of them were sentenced to be hung, and the others have already been executed. Soon it will be his turn."

"Jesus Christ!" exclaimed Masters. "Isn't there anything that can be done?"

She shook her head. "I have the best lawyers and they have fought hard to keep him alive." Her face grew more taut. "But he is guilty," her hands rose helplessly, "and there is no defense for guilt."

"But he is just a kid."

She nodded. "Yes, only a boy. But old enough to kill - and be killed."

He saw that she was about to break down, so he quickly attempted to distract her attention from Ichiro. "What about Hiroko? Does she feel the same about Americans?"

"I do not know, Keith. Sometimes I am not sure that I know Hiroko. We are very close and she is a wonderful daughter, but at times she has a - fierceness, which I cannot understand. Like the unpleasant way she spoke to you at our house. She should have realized that you came to help us, and that it took courage to face the family of a man who was killed by your soldiers."

"She had a right to ask who killed her father."

"Thank you for saying it. You are a gentle, perceptive man. But she had no right to ask it the way she did. It showed a lack of respect."

Masters smiled. "We are a different generation, Kimiko. She is from the new world."

"No Japanese girl should show disrespect, modern or not."

"Tell me," he asked. "Why have you never remarried? Is it because you were never certain about your husband?"

Color raced up into her face. "No," she replied. "All of us who lost dear ones knew that if they had not returned within a year or two after the war they were dead." She poured more tea into their cups. "I had no desire to remarry."

"I would think a beautiful woman like you would have to fight off the offers of marriage."

He drew back at the coldness which suddenly came into her face. She looked him straight in the eye. "How did you find my name and address?" she asked, bruskly.

"From the police."

"Then I am sure they informed you," she snapped, "that I was a registered prostitute for six years."

Masters sat motionless, staring into her icy eyes. Finally he looked away. "You didn't have to take out the family skeletons for me. Each of us has our own crosses to bear."

Her face grew more taut. "Come on, Mr. Masters, do not play games with me. You were in Japan during the Korean War. What did you do here?"

Masters remained silent.

"Well?" she demanded. "How many peasant girls from the countryside did you buy on the corners?"

His expression hardened. "Stop whipping yourself. Everything is for sale."

"Then let us stop pretending with each other. You know that a peasant girl does not own fine stores and home and car without having earned it in the one and only way that was permitted here." Then she let him have it with both barrels. "I also know," she hissed, "that it was you who killed Ito! You, and only you!"

Masters stiffened in his chair. Abruptly, she rose from her seat and walked out. He remained at the table for a few more moments, pensive, then paid the check and went outside. He was surprised to find the car still there, Kimiko seated behind the wheel, staring straight ahead. When Masters got in, she immediately drove off.

He remained silent for a long mile. "I had hoped you wouldn't guess," he finally said.

She said nothing, just kept her eyes fixed on the road. Then she sighed, deeply, as if everything was a bad dream and that one must sometime awaken and face reality. "I cannot condemn you. It was war. But I condemn the loss of a wonderful man, and I am bitter because my children were never able to feel his love. Perhaps if he had not died, Ichiro would be a happy boy in the university instead of a poor, terrified criminal waiting to have his valuable life snuffed out."

He turned towards here. "Kimiko, I will accept the responsibility for your husband's death, but believe one thing - I wounded him only. I don't know whether my shots would have caused his death or not, for as he lay there, one of my men shot him again."

The car abruptly swerved and she trod on the brakes. Carefully, she brought it to the side of the road and stopped. Then she laid her head on the steering wheel and wept.

Masters took her by the shoulder. "Crying won't change anything."

She pushed open the door and got out and began walking slowly by the side of the road. He sat until she became a small figure in the distance, then he left the car and followed her. After a while, he saw her turn back, and soon they met.

She stopped directly in front of him and met his eyes squarely. "Keith, why did you come to Japan?"

"I guess it was an attempt to atone for my sin. I could have stopped the final shot, but I didn't."

"Why did you not stop it?"

"I don't know, Kimiko. I've asked myself that question a score of times, without an answer."

"But why did you wait until now to come here?"

He shrugged. "I told you I have a heart condition, but understand that I may die at any time during another attack. Then it became important to find out about him, and you, while I was still able to."

She studied his face carefully. "And now?"

He pursed his lips. "I guess I'll go back home and wait to die," he said gruffly. "Then I'll find out."

"Is there absolutely no one waiting for you there?"

"Only death."

Their eyes met and locked. She took a step nearer and looked deeper into them, searching for a hidden sign. Then her hands rose to his face and she stood on tiptoe to press her lips against his cheek.

A passing car blared its horn in amusement as he reached out and swept her into his arms.

CHAPTER 4

Kimiko drove straight to Master' hotel and parked the car. "Would you like to come to supper at my home?" she asked.

"Yes. I'd like that. What time should I come?"

She glanced at her watch. "It is almost seven. Why don't you rest for an hour and I will have Hiroko pick you up at eight o'clock."

"Okay."

"Keith," she called, as he stepped out of the car. "Please do not mention our conversation to her. She does not know - about me."

He leaned in through the window. "Neither do I." They smiled at each other. "How about speaking of Ichiro?"

"Perhaps it should be avoided as much as possible. They were very close, and Hiroko is not quite - predictable. I will tell her I have spoken of him to you."

He nodded and strode into the hotel. Up in his room, he lay on his bed and thought about the boy. What a goddamn mess, he reflected. I need this aggravation like a first class migraine attack. If I had any sense, I'd get on a boat tonight and show my heels to Japan. This atonement crap is just a pipedream, a dramatic interlude to impress George Brighton between my waking up to reality and dropping dead from a crummy heart.

And now I am acting like a country schoolboy, holding hands with a pint-sized whore who has been screwed by half the army in Korea and thinking of a baked-brain kid who had nothing better to do than murder people. I wonder how that little bastard did kill the union guy?

He suddenly realized that he was very weary, and in minutes he was fast asleep.

He awoke at the sound of a knock on the door. "Who's there?" he called out.

"Hiroko."

Masters looked at his watch. It was eight o'clock. "I'll be right down." He rose quickly, poured tepid water from a jug into a porcelain bowl, washed, and in a few minutes was down in the lobby. Hiroko was not there, so he walked outside and found her sitting in Kimiko's car parked directly in front of the hotel.

"Sorry. I must have overslept," he said.

"That's all right." She started the engine and moved promptly into the traffic. "Did you enjoy yourself at my grandparents' home?"

"Yes."

At a traffic light she stopped and glanced at him. "Mother said that you have a bad heart. Also, that I am to apologize for speaking so disrespectfully."

Masters could hardly keep his eyes from the girl. She fascinated him with her strange, sensuous beauty. Experience had taught him that the girl knew it, too. He pulled himself away from his thoughts to answer her. "I assume that you are apologizing only because your mother ordered you to."

The traffic light changed and she started off. "Yes," she replied, with Kimiko's directness of speech.

"I don't accept it," he said, deciding to join battle. Her head swung round at his brusk refusal. "I am a stranger to you and your mother, and I don't want to interfere with Japanese customs. So far as I am concerned, you had the right to ask your questions in the way you did. If your mother feels different, then that is between you and her. I just won't accept an apology that is not really meant as one. So let's not make a federal case of it. Forget it."

Her brow wrinkled further. She drove in silence, attempting to comprehend his abrupt retort. Her eyes flicked at him. "You are a much harder man than I thought," she finally said. He let the remark pass unanswered. Then she flashed an open smile at him. "Okay, Mr. Masters, I apologize for myself, not because mother ordered me to do so."

Masters grinned back. "I accept it on the condition that you say it without smiling. You're a fine looking woman, and the smile makes the words too easy to accept."

She chuckled. "I guess that's meant as a compliment."

"You can take it as one."

The traffic had thinned out and she sped through the streets. "Mother likes you," she commented after a few minutes. He did not reply to her probe. From the corner of his eye he saw from the expression on her face that she was considering another tack. "Where did you stay?" she asked casually.

"At your grandparents' house?" he said easily, chuckling to himself. He decided to take a shot at her. "Are you trying to learn if we shared the same sleeping mat?"

Her reaction was not what he anticipated. Her face grew taut and her breasts visibly swelled. She swallowed. "My mother is a very beautiful and desirable woman." He decided not to answer her, just looked out of the window. But Hiriko would not be put off. "Well, did you?" she demanded boldly.

"Did we what?" asked Masters, enjoying himself tremendously.

Her breathing was noticeably heavy. "Did you share the same mat?"

He turned towards her. She was driving slowly, her eyes bright, her breasts rising and falling with excitement. He was suddenly aware that if he placed a hand on the girl, she would explode.

"Don't get any false notions, Hiroko," he said harshly. "Your mother took me to the countryside to show me what life was like many years ago. We barely know each other. Don't try to read a big romance into it."

She did not appear to have heard him, or, if she did, it made no impact. "What is it like," she asked tensely, "for middle-aged people to have an affair?"

He almost laughed out loud. Under her words, he sensed a direction she was aiming for that had nothing to do with the comments thus far. "Lay off, Hiroko," he said quietly.

A flush rose to her face. "Don't treat me as a child!" she snapped. "I know what it's all about."

So I was right, he decided. She wants to play games. His loins suddenly grew warm. "Fine. Then wait a few more years and you'll have all your questions answered about middle-aged people."

She held back her resentment at his remark. "What is it, a big secret?" she asked, her eyes staring straight ahead. "What would it be like if - say, a middle-aged man had an affair with a younger woman?"

Well, there it is, thought Masters. If I run now, then this utterly desirable woman-child would have the evil eye on me forever.

"She wouldn't satisfy him," he lashed out at her. "It would be just a tangle of arms and legs and sweat on the stomach. And he wouldn't satisfy her either. He'd be too old. Now, stop this crap and let's get home."

She turned startled eyes on him, as if he had slapped her face, as if he had rejected her. Then her mouth snapped shut and her foot slammed down on the accelerator.

As Masters reached the door to the house, it opened. Kimiko was standing there with a tall, straight-backed Japanese. At first glance, Masters told himself that this man, about sixty years old, was one very tough person.

"Good evening," said Kimiko, bowing in greeting. She turned to the tall, hard-faced Japanese. "Admiral, I would like to introduce you to Mr. Masters from the United States, who is visiting Japan. Mr. Masters, this is Admiral Kowasachi."

The Japanese took in all the details about Masters with one swift look, then he bowed very slightly, almost just a nod. Masters knew enough about Japanese customs to recognize this as tantamount to an insult. The deeper one bowed, the more respect was being paid. Kowasachi offered none. Masters set his jaw and just acknowledged the greeting with a dip of his chin. The admiral bowed more fully to Kimiko, then without a word, he started down the path. A long, black, chauffeured Mercedes was waiting at the curb.

Once Masters stepped inside, Kimiko bowed again, as if they had not met for a few weeks or so. He found her old-fashioned manners bewitching.

"Who was that interesting fellow?" he asked.

"A friend of mine. He has given me some sound financial advice over the years."

"Speaking of friendship, do I bow now?" he asked, smiling.

Kimiko laughed and reached out a hand to shake his. "Good evening, Mr. Masters," she said, noticing her daughter about to enter behind him.

"Would you call me Keith?" he said, turning his head to include Hiroko. "I would feel more at ease."

Kimiko nodded. "I am called Kimiko," she said, keeping up the deception. She was beautiful, sheathed in a silk dress of forest green, with small emeralds dangling from her ears and a string of perfectly matched pearls around her throat. "Would you care for a juice before dinner?"

"No, thanks."

"Then please, sit here." She settled him at the head of the table and the wrinkled, old servant served the meal at once. Hiroko sat opposite him, seemingly subdued.

"Did you get any sleep?" asked Kimiko.

"I overslept. Hiroko had to awaken me."

The girl leaned forward. "Mr. Masters...Keith, do you mind very much if we talk some more about my father?"

"Look, I realize I'm perhaps the only person you may ever meet who could give you the facts, so don't be afraid to ask whatever you want - and as often as you want. And I will understand if you ask me to repeat myself a dozen times."

"Thank you," said Kimiko. "There are a thousand questions in my mind, but I do not know how to put them."

Hiroko laid down her eating sticks. "We bought every article we could find about Iwo Jima. Mother even visited a few of our people who had surrendered there. But you are the first American we have ever spoken to about it. What was it like?"

"My army regiment was sent there towards the end to assist in cracking the final defenses and in moping up. Then we prepared beach defenses, in the event your people tried to take back the island."

"But the details, Keith," insisted Hiroko. "We've read so much about the military action that we know it by heart, but the day to day details - we couldn't find them in a book. How did my fath...our people, and yours, eat and sleep, and get treatment when they became ill?"

"Well, I guess you know the meaning of mopping up. That's when the main fighting is over and there are still small groups hiding out. We would search for them, to protect our airplanes and supply points from hit and run attacks. Actually, one of your groups came out at night and went wild through an airfield tent area with rifles and sabers. They killed a number of men before they were driven off."

Hiroko pushed aside her bowls of pork and rice. "Did you really try to get our people to surrender?"

"Of course we did. It stands to reason that it's better than going into caves after them. Remember, the Japanese soldier was taught to fight to the end. That meant we would have to lose men going in after them.

"At Iwo Jima, we dug fox holes, strung barbed wire around the entire perimeter to prevent your soldiers from throwing grenades into our positions while we slept, then, during the daytime, we'd enter caves to flush out small bands. At night we would set up ambushes to deter them from forming into larger groups for a coordinated attack."

"How did you try to get our men to surrender?" asked Kimiko. "Did some of your soldiers speak Japanese?"

"We had some Nisei along, Japanese-Americans. They would accompany us on patrol whenever we located any of your people in a cave. Later on, we had help from some of your soldiers who had surrendered. They would speak to the hold-outs, to explain that we would not kill them, that we would treat them properly as prisoners."

"You mean," exclaimed Hiroko, her face flushed with disbelief, "that Japanese soldiers would help you?"

"Hiroko," said Masters. "There was much false propaganda during the war, that we would torture and kill prisoners. The best way to prove it is not true is to send in a prisoner himself. A lot of good men, perhaps even your own father, would still be alive if they were given the right opportunity to surrender."

"How large was the cave of my husband?" asked Kimiko.

"About five feet wide, six or seven feet long, maybe four or five feet high."

"That means he could not even stand up."

"Yes."

"Was there any food?"

"I don't know." He was pretty certain there would not have been much, if any at all.

"How about water?"

"There was very little water on Iwo. Just a few wells."

Kimiko stared at him, and her silence impressed Hiroko. "I suppose that is what you meant when you spoke of ambushes at night," she finally said.

"Yes."

"Tell us," insisted Hiroko.

"It isn't pleasant."

"We did not expect it to be," said Kimiko.

"All right. We would set up machine gun positions around a well. Then, whenever we found a trail or natural access to the well, we'd put in booby traps and flares, so that anyone walking along would hit the trip wire. They would either be caught by the booby trap or the flare would light up the area. Then we could see well enough to shoot."

"They must have been horribly thirsty," sighed Kimiko. Masters did not answer, for he knew that water consumed their thoughts night and day. "What did they do when they were ill or injured?"

"We found a hospital cave directly under our battalion perimeter. It had an opening just large enough for a man to crawl inside. We heard that your people slipped in and out before it was discovered."

"What did you do with the hospital when you found it?" asked Hiroko, grimly.

"We sent in a Japanese prisoner, but they wouldn't let him come back out. A little while later we located one of their air vents and blew it shut. Soon a naval man came out and attempted to negotiate."

"What did he want to negotiate?" interrupted the girl.

"That we should leave the area unguarded so they could come out and commit suicide."

"I don't believe it," said Hiroko angrily.

Kimiko shook her head. "It was the way of our soldiers, Hiroko." She turned to Masters. "What did you do?"

"We refused, of course. We agreed to allow them to commit suicide undisturbed, but we would not open the ring we had placed around the cave opening. That would have been foolish. They would have sneaked out at night and attacked us or escaped."

"Well, what happened?" prompted the girl.

"The navy man suddenly decided that he didn't want to go back into the cave, and we didn't force him to. He told us that the hospital had two more air vents, so we searched about until we located them and blew them shut. Soon afterwards, they came out, about forty or so."

"Is that all?" asked Hiroko, skeptically.

Masters turned to face her. "No, it isn't all," he stated, sternly. "We went into the cave later on and found that before surrendering, the doctor in charge had murdered the seriously ill with injections."

There was a profound silence. "Why? Why?" said Kimiko, weakly.

He shrugged. "I don't know, Kimiko. Because people are insane. When I was young and a soldier, I didn't even ask. Everything seemed normal. Fighting, killing, committing suicide - it was all an accepted thing. You should know that."

"Poor, poor Ito," said Kimiko. "Caught up in all this, struggling so hard to take his feet out of the mud of the paddies, working day and night to make a better place for us." Then she fell silent, thinking of Ichiro.

Masters understood. "What is going to happen next?"

"He has a month," she replied. Then she stood up, as if to signal an end to the speaking of death for the night. "Come, Keith, let me show you the garden."

He followed her through the sliding doors into a large garden enclosed by the same high, bamboo fence, with hooded lanterns illuminating the perfectly tended flower beds and the lawn. A number of stone benches were ranged around a pentagon shaped pond in the center. The evening was cool and Kimiko caught up a shawl from a bench to place around her shoulders. They walked quietly round the garden, breathing in the scent of the flowers and the night.

In the shadows, Masters took Kimiko by the shoulders and looked down into her sad eyes. "Try not to worry too much."

"That is impossible to do, Keith. My heart is so full of sorrow."

He bent his head and kissed her gently on her lips. She stood passively in his arms, although she returned the kiss. "I will go now," he said.

"Stay as long as you wish. I am not tired."

He looked at his watch. It was after eleven. "When shall we meet again?"

She smiled up at him. "Whenever you wish. I do not have to be treated like a young girl."

Kimiko would not permit him to return to the hotel by taxi. She sent Hiroko to back out the car from the garage.

"Would you like to meet me for lunch?" she asked, as they kissed goodnight.

"Sure. Shall I pick you up at the store?"

"No. Tomorrow I will be at my main office. I will give you the address before you leave. It will give some of my other employees something to talk about for the rest of the week. Goodnight, and rest well."

Hiroko eyed him as he climbed inside the car. Within a block or two, she said, "I saw you kiss mother in the garden."

"You must have a good pair of field glasses. Did you also hear me say directly after we kissed that her heart should not be full of sorrow?"

"No, I only observed. It was not a kiss of condolence."

"Only one kiss?" he said, his sense of humor at full enjoyment.

"I bet you kissed her again while I was getting the car."

Masters had to laugh. "It could have been a dozen or so. Do you think your mother needs someone to protect her?"

"She is a lonely woman. And your sudden arrival could be somewhat romantic, if one ignores the reason for you having come."

"I think your mother is an intelligent, down-to-earth person who wouldn't go jumping to conclusions like a certain young lady who is related to her."

Hiroko smiled. "Well, tell me the truth. Have you two gone further than kisses?"

"Why?" asked Masters, amused. "Would you like us to?"

"You didn't answer. You're evading the question."

"You first. Would you want us to?"

"No, I wouldn't want mother to have an affair with you."

"Why not?"

"It's your turn to answer. How about it?"

"We have not gone further than the kiss or two we spoke of."

"Do you intend to?"

"My God, you're a nosy person. It's none of your business. But let's get back to my question. Why wouldn't you like us to have an affair."

As soon as he asked it, Masters knew she had been leading him along, and he wished he could recall the question.

"Perhaps I'd like to have an affair with you myself," she replied, calmly.

He did not make the mistake of laughing. "No dice, Hiroko. You're playing with words, like some people play with explosives to learn how far they can go before it blows up."

"Why not. Am I not beautiful? Wouldn't you like to have a woman like me?"

"Nope."

"I don't believe you. I bet you'd like to touch me right now."

"Sure I would. I'd like to wring your neck. I told you to lay off. If you have hot pants, then find a nice young fellow."

"I've found nice, young fellows. They don't impress me."

"Then find an old one. But don't con me."

She pulled the car to the curb and stopped. The street was in darkness. She turned to face him. "Keith, don't speak to me with an old man to young girl attitude. First, you aren't an old man. Second, I'm a big girl where it matters, and you know it. You haven't stopped looking at me since we met. A man likes to make love to a woman, especially good-looking ones. Please be serious. Why won't you make love to me if I ask?"

He knew he had to answer it carefully. If he screwed this one, he would have to leave Japan at once. It would be the end of his highfalutin ideas about atonement, the friendship he felt for Kimiko, the first enjoyment he had had in so many years. "Not every man wants to sleep with every beautiful woman he sees," he said. "When you're young and have hot pants, that's another matter. You tussle around in bed, and when it's over, you have a good laugh, go out for a drink, then go home feeling like you met a good friend. Later on in life, you learn that complications set in if you try to act like a kid." He stopped short because he realized he had made a mistake.

Hiroko knew it, too. "I dare you to take me to a hotel right now and let me get undressed. I bet you'd eat your words."

"For Christ's sake," snorted Masters. "What's all the talk about? If you want to get laid, find somebody who's in the mood and do it. Leave me out of it. Now, get the car on the road."

For a moment he thought she was going to open her blouse and expose herself and all his brave talk. Perhaps she had enough sense to know that the car was too small. Anyhow, she started the motor and drove off.

"You're bluffing," she said. "I'm taking you to a hotel to find out. If after I get undressed, you tell me to get out, I'll do so and never bother you again."

"Like hell you will. Drive me to my hotel or I'll take a goddamn taxi."

"Afraid?" she hissed.

"Not of you running bare-assed around a room, but I am of complications - and you are a headache if ever I saw one. Now shut up and take me to my hotel."

When the car pulled up, he got out quickly. "Keith," she called. He bent down to the window, drawing in his breath at her beauty. "I'll bet that one day you will make love to me. And for the rest of your life, you'll never forget it."

Then she slipped the car into gear and sped off.

He stood for a moment at the curb, watching the taillights fade, wondering if the fire in his loins would allow him to get to sleep that night.

CHAPTER 5

The following day, Masters took a taxi to Kimiko's office. It was a modern, white brick building, three stories high, in a less commercialized section, but still high caliber. He saw the same Japanese characters on the front as was on her main store, and it struck him that he had seen the same characters on another store en-route. That must have been another one of her chain. As he entered, a receptionist promptly rose and bowed. A quick glance of that floor showed eight or nine women working on books and invoices, and three cubicles along one wall for more women on phones - apparently buyers.

From the receptionist's eagerness to lead him up a flight of stairs, it was obvious that he was expected. The next floor had nine or ten women on sewing machines, and racks of women's wear along the rear. It seemed as though Kimiko was making some items especially for her own chain. The third floor was ultra modern, glass-enclosed offices for other workers, and ceiling high leather doors leading into a large office at the rear. Two men were seated in the entry, apparently waiting to speak with someone.

The receptionist turned Masters over to a tall, slender woman, evidently Kimiko's secretary, who unobtrusively pressed a button while rising to bow.

Kimiko came out at once, and even across the room he could see an unusual brightness in her eyes. She bowed, then led him into her office. It was twice the size of the one in her store, of chrome and leather, with shelves filled with catalogues. Once inside, she kissed him lightly on the lips.

"Say," he exclaimed. "What a place you have. And what gives with the kiss?"

She guided him to leather sofa and sat down beside him. "I thought of you most of last night," she confessed, "and I was glad to see you again."

Masters chuckled.

"Would you like to eat here in the office?" she asked.

"I've no objection, but one of these days I'll have to start paying for my meals instead of sponging on you."

"You are not imposing, Keith. I enjoy it. And it is foolish to pay restaurant prices if you do not have to. My girls have a kitchen downstairs, and it is no trouble to cook a meal."

He looked at her again, and it struck him what a helleva women she was, not just because she was watching out for his pocketbook, or that she might someday end up in bed with him, but by virtue of the unquestionable honesty and warmth which she exuded.

He rose. "I'll be right back."

He strode out of the office, down the two flights of stairs, and walked a couple of blocks until he came to a flower shop he had passed on the way to the office. There he purchased a small bouquet. The smiles of the receptionist and secretary became broad grins as, red-faced, he went by them up the stairs and back into the office. Without a word he handed Kimiko the bouquet, suddenly aware of the fact that it was the first time in his life he had ever given flowers to a woman.

Although Japan was a country of flower-giving, to her the silent gesture seemed significant. She gazed long and hard at him. "These have a special meaning, haven't they, Keith?" she finally said.

"Just a gift," he answered, beginning to feel a little foolish.

Her eyes remained steadfast. "You don't have to court me to prove anything."

"I'll try not to, then."

A thoughtful smile played around her lips as she went to a bookcase, opened a door at the bottom, and took out a slender, exquisite vase, filled it with water, and slowly arranged the flowers. "They are very beautiful. You have chosen well," she told him.

He sat down. "This romance business is reserved strictly for kids," he said flatly. He reached out a stubby forefinger to the perfectly arranged flowers and pushed one of them out of line. "Leave them like this," he ordered. "Everything in the world is a little cock-eyed anyhow."

Her eyes were still smiling as she left the office to order their lunch.

When they finished eating, she motioned to the sofa. "Why don't you lie down and rest a while?"

"I'm not tired," he objected. "Look, this heart business hasn't made an invalid of me. I'm just as good as the next guy. I'm just not supposed to mix cement or carry pianos upstairs."

Within a few minutes he learned that the stories about Japanese women being docile were strictly rumors. She brooked no argument. Soon his jacket was hanging in the closet and he was lying on the couch with a western style pillow under his head.

"This book," she said, taking a bound volume from a drawer, "says that you should rest after meals."

"When did you become a medical expert?"

"This morning," she replied with a grin. "What do you have?"

"Angina pectoris."

"Where are your pills - what do you call them?"

"Nitroglycerine. In my jacket pocket."

She got the bottle and placed it by the sofa. "You must always keep them at hand."

He chuckled, delighted with her ministrations. "Okay, doc. What does the book say about you coming down here and kissing the patient?"

She dropped to her knees and kissed him, another of her fleeting touch of lips. Then she sat on the floor by the couch.

"Tell me about yourself, Keith."

"Me?" He laughed. "It would put you to sleep."

"No, seriously, tell me."

He knew what she was after. All women wanted to know the same thing. "I was married twenty years ago. Was divorced - Christ, it's been nine years now. Have a son a few years younger than Ichiro."

"What is he like?"

"Bert? I really don't know. I haven't seen him since the divorce."

"Oh, no, your own son. Why haven't you seen him?"

"He didn't want to see me. His mother was pretty bitter and some of it rubbed off on him."

"I'm sure he would like to see you again."

"I wouldn't bet on that. I'd lose."

"And your wife. Did you love her?"

"I thought I did. I don't know whether I did love her or not. I do know that I wish I had never married her."

"You must have loved her to get married."

"That's a cliché, Kimiko, and I bet every guy who steps before the divorce court hears it a couple of thousand times."

"Did you ever love another woman besides your wife?"

"No, but I was fond of a few others."

She seemed to grow still. "It is strange, but in the few days since I have know you, I have felt...well, a greater interest in things."

"A lot can happen in a few days, Kimiko. I've known people who died in a split second. Why can't others wake up to personal feelings as quickly."

She rested her head against his shoulder. "Yes, they should be able to. I wish I were as certain about things as you are."

He grinned wryly as a thought abruptly struck. "I can afford to be certain. When you don't know how much time you have left, you can take all the chances you want."

"You are a good man. You understand so many things and are not afraid to stand by your convictions. I always have doubts."

"You seem to be pretty sure of things to have built up the company like you have." That reminded him of another matter. He sat up. "There must be an answer for Ichiro. Is there no further appeal possible?"

She shook her head, sorrowfully. "No, we have been through them all."

"Won't his age help towards a commutation of the sentence?"

"There were two boys younger than Ichiro. It did not make any difference in their cases. Oh, Keith, I would give my life gladly if I could help him."

He rose and looked down on her sitting on the floor, a small, slender form, bowed with grief. He helped her rise, then went to the closet and took his jacket.

"Where does Hiroko spend her days?" he asked.

"She works for the Economic Division. She is a graduate economist."

He grinned at the affection in her voice. "You are proud of her, aren't you?"

"Oh, yes. She is a lot like my husband. When she makes up her mind about something, she does not stop until she gets it."

"Where does she work?"

"On Harumi-Dori Avenue."

"Does she know anyone in the government who could help?"

"No, I am afraid not. Knowing someone does not help in this case."

He kissed her. "I'll take off now."

"Will you come to supper tonight?"

"I'll be there." He descended to the street and hailed a taxi. The Economic Division was back towards the Ginza District, and directly inside the main door he found an information desk. The receptionist knew Hiroko.

She came trotting down to the entrance in a few minutes. "Hi, Keith," she greeted him, surprised at his appearance. "Want to go to a hotel now?"

In spite of himself, he had to chuckle. "Not yet, Hiroko." He looked round. "Can you get off work for a while?"

"Sure." She studied him closely. "Is something wrong?"

"No, but let's go to a quiet corner."

She led him outside and down the street to a small restaurant. They took a table at the rear and ordered cokes.

"Hiroko, give me all the information you have about Ichiro."

Her face fell. "Poor Ichiro. He joined the Communist Party about two years ago. He told me about it, but I had to promise not to say anything to mother. He really hated you Americans. I guess that's why he joined. The Party was trying to get into a union of clerks, so they supported one of the delegates who was running for election as the head of the union. When he was elected, the Party insisted that he select some of their people as his assistants. He refused. Ichiro told me that they were going to beat him up as a warning, but shortly afterwards there was an announcement over the television that the union leader was found stabbed to death.

"Ichiro was very nervous for the next couple of days, then one night he confessed to being one of the group who had stabbed the official. I gave him all the money I had and he left home to go into hiding. I think he intended to stay in the countryside with some of father's relatives, but the police arrested him before he could get away.

"At the trial, they produced two witnesses who saw the murder and who identified the entire group. There were five boys. Ichiro said that the Party passed them orders in jail to say nothing, so they didn't even confess and plead for mercy. The other four were executed over six months ago. Mother has been spending scads of money on appeals, but they've all been turned down."

"Are you sure there is no further appeal possible?"

She shook her head. "We have one of the best attorneys in Tokyo, the kind who would fight right up to the end, and even he has given up."

"Is there absolutely no chance for a commutation of his sentence?"

"Not since the others have been executed. The lawyer said the only reason he's stayed alive this long is because mother has spent so much on appeals, and that it would be a great scandal if they commuted his sentence now - as if money bought it."

He called the waiter to the table. "Tell him to bring me a pack of cigarettes," he ordered Kimiko.

"I thought you weren't supposed to smoke."

"Do as you're told," he growled. When he lit the first cigarette, his head spun and his mouth burned. He drew in another lungful, thinking hard. Hiroko sat quietly, watching him.

"Exactly how much time before the execution?" he finally asked.

"Thirty-four days."

"Where is he held?"

"At the Tokyo Central Prison. It's on the northwest side, about half an hour away by taxi. Do you want to go there?"

He shook his head. "Listen, Hiroko, I may want you to help me with a few things. But before we start, I want you to get this screwing around business out of your mind. Do you understand?"

"You want to sleep with me. I can tell it, now."

"For Christ's sake, can't you listen when somebody wants to talk to you."

"Then why make such a big case out of it. Let's go to a hotel and have one affair. Then it will be over and done with." She leaned forward. "I'm not kidding, Keith. It's really important to me." When he opened his mouth to answer, she cut him off. "Look at me. Look closely. Wouldn't you like to see what I am like underneath?"

He rose from his chair, upsetting the empty coke glasses, and strode out into the street. Quickly, he walked a couple of blocks, then looked back to see if she was following. He leaned against the side of a building and puffed as if he had run a great distance, but it did not help. He loins felt as if they would burst in the middle of the street. He walked another block to cool off, cursing this girl who affected him so strongly.

Kimiko called for him at seven. "How come you are driving?" he asked. "I thought you would send Hiroko."

"She has drawing classes every Monday evening."

"So, tonight's the night," he quipped. "Where do I attack you, in the living room or in the garden?"

She pinched his thigh playfully. "Would you not rather see a Japanese Kabuki play?"

"Are you kidding?" said Masters, breaking into a laugh.

"No. There is a very old-fashioned one tonight. I would like to take you after supper." He groaned. "What is the matter? Do you not like them?"

"Frankly, I've never seen one, but I've heard about them and the music. I will go, but you will have to drag me."

She chuckled. "I intend to, for I know you will enjoy it. I know the words and music are not pleasant to Western ears, but the important parts of the show are the movements of the actors' hands and feet. Each motion has a special meaning, and the audience must guess what the actors are trying to say. It is like a quiz game. Do you not feel wonderful when you are able to answer a question?"

"If it's a hard one."

"That is exactly it - in the show. The actor says or sings certain words and the audience knows what each movement means, but putting them together to express an idea is what makes it so interesting. I will explain some of the motions before we go, then you can tell me whether you understand it."

"I am already confused."

"It is not too hard, Keith. Look, see the way I turn my hand?"

"Yes, and I think you turn it with great distinction."

"You are hopeless," she chided him, fondly. "Now, seriously, watch my hand." She rotated it. "That means everything is going wrong. When I wiggle it like this, it means you should leave. And when I hold it like this, it means a bicycle. Now, if I make the three movements, what would it suggest?"

He thought for a few seconds. "That something is wrong with the bicycle and that I should leave."

"That is very good for a start. Actually, in the sequence I showed you, it means that everything is going wrong and that you leave with or on the bicycle. What makes it more amusing is that the actor is also saying things by mouth and with his feet, and they must all be taken together. It is surprising what funny things he can express."

"How the devil do you learn all that?"

"Oh, it takes some time to know it well. When an actor performs for children, he does very simple things, like a goat butting a bad man, or an evil spirit being caught in a bottle. They love it, and learn as they go along come with me, you will enjoy it."

During supper, Masters told her that he had spoken to Hiroko to learn more of the facts about Ichiro. "Do you mind if I speak to your attorney, too?" he asked.

"I would be happy if you did. Sometimes it is difficult for me to understand all those legal terms."

"Does he speak English?"

"I do not think so. I will be glad to interpret for you."

"No, not you. There's enough misery for you in just thinking about Ichiro."

"How about Hiroko? She can take time off from work whenever she wants."

"All right. I'll ask her."

She stretched out her hand and placed it over his. "Have you thought of anything which might be of help?"

He shook his head. "I'm no lawyer, so don't build any false hopes. I just want to discuss it with him and get as many facts as I can."

After supper, they drove to the theater. It was situated in a narrow alley, and parked around it were a number of new, expensive automobiles. Masters paid the two thousand, eight hundred yen admission fee, then they entered a rectangular hall dimly lit by candle lanterns hanging from the ceiling. A wide aisle ran from the stage to the rear of the theater. The seats were long, hard, wooden benches, set so close together that even his average height made him feel huge among the Japanese. When he sat down, his knees drove into the back of the man seated in front of him. He apologized and turned sideways to avoid a recurrence.

He was surprised to see how well-dressed the audience was.

"This theater is for the people of this section," explained Kimiko in a low voice. "There is another downtown for the poorer people."

After a while, the candle lanterns were pulled up higher to dim the interior. Masters peered apprehensively at their proximity to the ceiling, visualizing the mad dash for the exits if one of them should set the old building on fire.

The curtain opened. The entire front of the stage was illuminated by a row of clean-burning candles. "Why do they use candles instead of electric lights?" he whispered to Kimiko.

"Custom," she whispered back. "In the villages there was no electricity. It would not be the same if they used electric lights."

A tall, heavy man in a flowing silk robe, wearing a dragon's mask, came out and bowed to the audience. They applauded politely. Then a short, slender man, also dressed in silk, his face painted a startling white with black rings around his eyes and hair drawn to the top of his head in a knot, entered the stage and bowed. The audience nearly tore the theater apart with its applause.

"He is Kazuo Yamagata, the most famous pantomimic in Japan," explained Kimiko, vigorously clapping her hands.

Suddenly, the actor in the dragon's mask took up a stance and his hand moved. A deathly hush enveloped the audience. From one side of the theater came the nerve-jarring wail of a flute. Everyone leaned forward. Masters glanced at Kimiko. Her eyes were glued to the stage and her lips were open, like a child watching a marionette show.

The masked actor made a series of movements and uttered a number of sing-song words. Masters nudged Kimiko. "Did he just make the motion for house?"

She grasped his hand. "Good, my dear. He is saying that a dragon is circling the house of the old man, waiting for him to come out." Her eyes immediately turned back to the stage. Suddenly the audience began to laugh.

"What happened?" he whispered.

"The old man says he smelled night soil."

Masters realized that he had been watching the dragon only. His eyes began shifting from actor to actor. A few minutes later the audience roared. The old man had made a movement of his hand and foot. He made the movement again, realizing that some of the audience had not yet understood. The roof nearly went off the building.

Kimiko, tears in her eyes, dragged her attention away to whisper, "He says that he had made a mistake about the odor. It was not night soil, but the tax collector."

Then the audience began hissing. "The dragon is going to wait until the old man is asleep to attack him," said Kimiko, actually enraged. Masters almost laughed aloud at how seriously she was taking it.

As the play continued, he found himself recognizing a few of the words and gestures Kimiko had shown him before coming to the theater, but was unable to relate them to the play.

Finally, after over an hour, the old man spun, clapped his hands, and the dragon fell to the floor. The audience broke into smiles, cheering, standing up to clap their hands. The old man and the dragon came to the edge of the stage and bowed, acknowledging the applause which lasted a good five minutes. Then the candle lanterns were lowered from the ceiling and the packed crowd made its way out.

Arm in arm, Kimiko and Masters walked the two blocks to the car. She was still smiling. "It is not easy to explain, Keith, as the story is a series of episodes. It is like that comedian you have, Bob - Bob."

"Bob Hope."

"Yes. I saw him one time, and although I could understand the words, I was not able to appreciate his humor. The American audience, however, went into hysterics."

"I understand."

"Would you mind going again?" she asked, drawing closer to him.

He felt her breast press against his arm, and knew it would be no great hardship to put up with events like tonight if it brought her such pleasure.

"No," he replied, and was surprised to learn that he really meant it.

When they reached the house, she asked if he wanted some tea.

"I'd like some air," he said. "Let's go into the garden. That candle smoke was heavy."

She took his arm and they strolled over the soft grass.

"It is so peaceful here together," she said, leaning her head against his shoulder.

"Yes," he agreed. "I feel more content than I've ever been before. In America, it was rush, rush, all the time rush. A half-hour for gulping down a sandwich, working in the evenings, sitting glued to the television set like it was a drug. Never the time for a peaceful walk on the grass, breathing in fresh air, not giving a damn that each moment is passing by and being lost forever."

"Is each moment really lost forever?"

"Yes. But now each moment seems to replace a year of what I once called living. I was always waiting for tomorrow, or something to come, or something to be gained, or something to be faced. As if there was never really a now, a this-very-instant. All of a sudden, I'm beginning to live consciously, as if everything is happening right now. I take this step - and it is right now. And when I speak of the step I have just taken, it is not an action of a few seconds ago, but a part of right now. It's because you are here with me, Kimiko."

She walked along quietly for a few steps. "You feel deeply about me," she finally said. Her head turned towards him and her eyes probed for his in the shadows. "Does what you feel about me use up those precious moments?" she asked softly.

He shook his head. "A week ago I would have said yes. Maybe even three days ago - or yesterday. But not now."

"I am sorry?" she murmured.

"What for?"

She took a deep breath. "I think you want me. But I am not ready."

He smiled. "Of course I want you. But maybe this is love and we both don't know how to accept it. But I do feel that you are waiting for something, and I think I know what it is."

She stopped him in the light of a lantern so she could see his eyes. "What is it, Keith? I do not know myself."

He looked steadily at her. "You know I was in Tokyo during the Korean operation. And we both know the hotels the officers used to stay at, and the corners we would pass in the evenings, and the barrooms full of girls with their eyes operated on." Her head drooped, but he forced up her chin so she had to face him. "You're purifying yourself, Kimiko. I know you don't have to, but you think differently. It's important to you, so do it in your own time and your own way - and don't worry about me in the interim."

She pressed her head against his chest, and he sensed her struggle for words. "Hush, hush," he whispered, kissing her hair. And she remained quiet.

Lester Taube

CHAPTER 6

It was Wednesday afternoon before an appointment could be made with Ichiro's attorney. Master took no chances by arranging to meet Hiroko in front of the building directly before the meeting.

"You've been avoiding me," she greeted him, accusingly.

"I've been avoiding you because I have no desire to have anything to do with you," he snapped back. He was already on the defensive and sore as hell that he was making a hash of his explanation. "Come on," he growled, cutting off her reply. "Or we'll be late."

The attorney, Mr. Takahashi, was a plump man of about sixty, courteous to the point of subservience, but who did not waste a moment once the introduction formalities were concluded. Without referring to notes, he gave a concise history of the case, and concluded with the statement that the sentence of death had been expected from the start, and each appeal had only been a delaying action.

"The best I had hoped for," he explained, "was a series of errors in court procedure upon which I could base a request for a new trial. If only the boy had admitted that the conspiracy was communist controlled and had cooperated with the police, there might have been the possibility of a long prison term instead of the death sentence. His accomplices, although two of them were younger, had a number of prior convictions, and the court took this into consideration. But Ichiro could have pleaded extenuating circumstances, and we could have fought for a mitigation of his sentence."

"Could he now cooperate and hope for a commutation?" asked Masters.

The attorney sighed. "No. I am fully convinced that it would change nothing - that his cooperation at this late date would only increase public opinion against him. The principal problem, Mr. Masters, is the manner of homicide. In Japan, death is rarely imposed upon a murderer except in instances of multiple victims. However, in this case the victim was stabbed over forty-seven times in a horrendous exhibition of brutality." He sighed again. "I have already had a meeting with the Minister of Justice, pleading for a last-minute reprieve, but it was useless. I have an appointment for another appeal at the middle of next week, and it was obtained on the premise that I would present new evidence, which I actually do not possess." Masters then heard the remark which indicated the measure of the man. "I must keep fighting for this boy's life, if only to enable him, in future years, to repay a part of the debt he owes society."

"Is there anyone higher up in the government who can be appealed to?" insisted Masters.

"No. I have already overstepped the bounds of propriety by speaking to the Minister of Justice. Japanese law is very strict in that the courts must not be circumvented. Any further steps in that direction would be met with resentment and would not assist us in this case."

"How will he die?" Masters saw the shock on Hiroko's face when he asked her to pose the question.

"By hanging," replied the attorney.

"Is there no possible way of delaying the execution - at least for a little longer."

The lawyer leaned back into his chair. "The courts are not vindictive, Mr. Masters," he explained. "On the contrary, obtaining stays of execution in Japan is encouraged whenever the slightest new information might have some bearing upon the case, even if it would not really affect the final judgment. We have already tried the patience of the court by a number of somewhat irresponsible appeals. The attitude of the court is not that it wants its pound of flesh, but that all possibilities have been exhausted and that justice should be done."

"How is the boy taking it?"

"He is frightened and makes no attempt to conceal it. He is also resigned to dying, but he is sad that his family and friends have been disgraced by his actions. Most important, he is aghast by the fact that he has taken a life, regardless of the circumstances. I firmly believe that with his present understanding, he would choose death for himself rather than take a life again, even if he could avoid retribution."

There was nothing more to be said. Masters and Hiroko left the attorney's office and walked down the street, silent, deep in thought. He stopped in the middle of the block.

"Hiroko, that fellow I met at your house - Admiral Kowasachi. What is his relationship to the family?"

"He has been seeing mother for about two years now." She cocked her head to study him. "It is not what you think. Mother has not had any relationship with a man since father."

Kimiko had certainly concealed her past life successfully, thought Masters. He wondered how she explained her eye operations. Probably that it helped her business with Americans, in the event she did business with them. "What do you mean, 'not what I think?' Are you a mind reader?"

"I know your nature."

"Well, smartass, what I was thinking was whether he had any pull. After all, he is an admiral."

"He has a lot of pull. He's not only just a former admiral, but he also owns some very large companies. Mother said she asked him once. He replied that nobody can help. It would bring down any government that tried."

In spite of himself, Masters had to ask the question. "Why does he see your mother?"

Hiroko chuckled. "I knew you would get around to that. Mother says he gives her financial advice, but I think she interests him sexually. After all, not many women in Japan have built up a business as large as Mother's, and the idea would attract many men. In addition, I'm sure you've noticed that she is a beautiful woman."

"I've noticed."

"He is a very tough person. A lot like you." She straightened up and thrust out her breasts a little further.

"He has looked at me like he would enjoy a romp in bed."

"There's your chance. He's old, tough, and available."

"He doesn't intrigue me. You do."

Masters shook his head with disgust. If only he learned to keep his mouth shut, maybe they could hold a conversation that made sense. "Look, Hiroko, let's get to a more important subject. You will have to help your mother during the next few weeks. You will have to try harder than ever before in your life to give her consideration and hope."

Hiroko sighed in resignation. "But how, Keith? How can I tell her to replace the memory of Ichiro with something else? What can I give her in exchange?"

He eyed her closely. "Have you ever thought of marrying? Of having children? Grandchildren would lessen some of the sadness."

She stood quietly, gnawing her lower lip thoughtfully. "Will you marry me, Keith?" she finally asked.

He knew instinctively that she was deadly serious. "No. First of all, grandchildren with blue eyes and brown hair would not be Ichiro. Secondly, I don't want to marry you."

"Is it because you are in love with Mother?"

"That's none of your business. Your entire concept of us is idiotic. You must get this absurd fixation out of your head."

She shook her head. "You're saying it, but you really don't believe it. It isn't idiotic, Keith. You're the one who is blind. You are looking only at twenty years difference in our ages." She took his hand. "Keith, you would not be good for Mother." When he opened his mouth to reply, she pulled on his hand. "Please, hear me out. Mother is essentially old Japan, and you would soon tire of what is now a novelty to you. She might enter into a relationship with you, but it wouldn't make her any more happy - and in truth, no more unhappy. If you had been raised in Japan, even though inherently a Westerner, you two would have a basis on which to build your happiness together.

"But you and I could find common ground, and much more to your advantage than you think. I don't know what kind of relationships you have had with other women, but I would surprise you. You wouldn't tire of me." Then she hit him where it hurt. "And you will need somebody like me. Tomorrow, next week, next year."

He felt like an imbecile, listening to this girl, being almost persuaded into conjuring up a picture of life with her. What the hell kind of an answer could a man give to a proposal made in the middle of the street from a girl who made his stomach tighten with a desire so strong that it actually hurt. But he could not pass it off lightly.

"It wouldn't work," was all he could think of saying.

Then this extraordinarily beautiful girl smiled. "It would work, Keith. I know it, because I know myself. You're a hard man, an independent kind of man who could do anything you really wanted to do. I'm like that, too. And you're soft and gentle at the right times. I know that when you make love to me, I will really feel like a woman. You'll be good for me, and it's not a father fixation which attracts me. I can make you happy. Do we have to make a shambles of Mother's life to find out?"

He sighed. "Hiroko, I'm fond of your mother, but you've got to understand that it doesn't mean we will become involved. Even if I had never met her, I still wouldn't want to become mixed up with a girl like you. You're full of complications - from A to Z."

She was neither offended nor sidetracked. Instead she kept attacking. "Does Mother love you?" she asked, certain of his reply.

"Of course not. We barely know each other. And I'm sure she has no inclination to start any kind of a romance."

"Like blazes, she doesn't," she snapped back, coolly. "I know Mother, perhaps better than she knows herself." She tapped his chest. "Did you ever sleep with a woman who loved you a little less than you loved her?"

"I guess so."

"How soon afterwards did you leave her?" Masters pursed his lips. The girl knew where to strike. "Listen, Keith," she pressed on. "With me, you'll be fighting every day for more of my love, and every day I'll give you more. It will never run out, and every night you'll go to sleep knowing that the next day you'll have more than the day before."

"Isn't it just a bit disloyal to interfere with your mother's feeling for the sake of your own?" He tried to become angry. "And goddamned selfish?"

"Want us to go and tell her that we want to live together and see what happens? I bet she heaves a sigh of relief. You've swept her off her feet, Keith. You think differently, that it all came by itself, but the truth is that you touched Mother in a sentimental spot. That doesn't mean you can live happily together for the rest of your lives. Mother needs a man from her own kind of people. He doesn't have to be a hill farmer, but he has to understand the subtleties of our way of life."

She tapped his chest again. "You two went to the theater a couple of nights ago. I'll bet Mother paid more attention to the performance than she did trying to explain it to you. How about it?"

"What the hell is that supposed to prove?" he replied, knowing full well what she was getting at, and realizing that she was right.

"Don't tell me she enjoyed it more trying to explain it to you than if she had attended it with a man of our own people who understood it."

"For Christ's sake," growled Masters. "Life is not just going to theaters or liking or disliking sukiyaki."

"It sure is, Keith, and I can see you are waking up to the fact that a kid half your age knows a little more than just the way to a bedroom. I'll make a deal with you. You spend a couple of nights with me and then I'll go away for a week. If, before that week is up, you don't come after me, I'll return and be the politest, most cooperative girl you've ever met - and I'll do all I can to help you and Mother."

He was ready to welcome another heart attack. He drew a deep breath. "Okay, Hiroko. We've talked it all out. I've heard you and I say, no dice. Now get the hell away from me or I'll smack your face."

She stared back at him defiantly. "You know I'm right," she stated flatly. "In fact, you want me this very minute, don't you?"

He slapped her face, hard. She reeled back from the unexpected blow, but kept her hands by her sides, refusing to raise one to her stinging cheek. She stepped closer, erect, proud, oblivious of the people stopping to stare.

"You want me badly, don't you, Keith," she said quietly.

He slapped her again, harder. She stumbled to the pavement, but got up immediately and moved back towards him.

He stood his ground for a few moments, then, acknowledging defeat, he turned and strode through the crowd that had collected, walking rapidly, almost at a trot, away from her. After a few blocks, he halted, panting, sweat trickling down his brow, and looked round. She had not followed.

He almost decided not to go to Kimiko's house for supper, but finally admitted that the situation must be faced or he would have to catch the first boat out of Japan. Kimiko was waiting outside the hotel at half past six.

"You seems tired, Keith," she observed with anxiety as he climbed inside the car.

He almost laughed. "It's been a long day." Glancing at her, he was suddenly filled with a great tranquility. "I should have rested after the meeting with Takahashi."

"Then you must lie down for a while before supper. I have a chaise lounge in the garage. We will put it in the garden for you to take a nap first."

He covered her hand on the steering wheel. "I'm all right, Kimiko. I don't have to be babied."

She turned soft eyes on him. "Please don't be offended, Keith, if I want to watch over you a little."

He smiled and leaned over to kiss her cheek. "I'm not really offended. Secretly, I enjoy being babied now and then."

"Good. Then I shall make a greater effort." Her voice faltered. "Hiroko came to the store and said Mr. Takahashi was unable to think of anything else to help Ichiro. Were you able to think of anything?"

"No." He hesitated. "Will you be able to face it?"

She sighed deeply. "We are not truly fatalists, we Japanese. Losing Ichiro will be losing the part of me that had more meaning and importance than anything else. I would be the happiest woman on this earth if I could give my life for his. And when he dies, I shall continue living - but food will not be as sweet nor the garden as restful. There will be nothing to work for, to build for."

"There is Hiroko."

"Yes, but she will have everything she needs."

"Some day she may have sons."

Kimiko had never thought of that. The implication suddenly struck her. "Yes," she said. "It would be good to hold a boy child in my arms again."

"See, you are a fatalist at heart."

She considered it carefully. "I guess we all are when it serves our purpose. But I cannot believe it when I think of Ichiro. I will never accept his death, not even at the ceremony for his ashes."

Masters steered her back to brighter thoughts. "Does Hiroko have a boy whom she likes?"

"No. She has many friends, but no-one has really appealed to her. I can understand that. She is a modern woman who is seeking more out of life than the women of my generation sought. One day she will find her man, and, like all of us, drift back to the comfortable ways of the generations before us."

"What do you mean by that?"

"Oh, the relationship between man and woman, the knowledge that a woman is happiest when she is giving all of her thoughts to her husband and children. That learning things, or having abilities, are of value only when they are devoted to the well-being of the family and not for the sake of the woman herself. Each generation goes through the same struggle, but when the girl is properly raised, she sooner or later reverts to the time-tested way of life."

"Obedience to the male?"

"No, love of being a woman - which is essentially the same if you look at it practically. I am sure every toiling farmer's wife in the countryside envies my fine business and house and freedom. They do not realize how much more I envy them."

"Isn't that somewhat prosaic?"

"What does it mean - this prosaic?"

"Dull, commonplace."

"Not at all, dear Keith. I speak for every happy woman in the world; let me wash the sweat and dirt from my husband's clothes, even in a cold mountain stream, and it is not labor, but an expression of love. Perhaps he has the facility to put it into words, or maybe he can show it only by his actions, such as looking at me fondly. It is the same. But what is all this living without it? Nothing."

"You've not conformed to the pattern."

"Yes, I have. I have Ito's love inside me. When I did things I was ashamed of, I did it for Ito's children, not only because I loved them, but because he did - and that was more important. When I worked hard to build up my stores, it was Ito's love that inspired me. It was not labor, ever." Her eyes misted. "Now I have failed him. His son was to grow straight and good and to have sons who would remember from whom they came."

"That's not your fault, Kimiko."

"Yes it is. I was left to do it, but I failed."

"There are still Hiroko's sons."

She lifted her chin. "That is true. They must do, then." She glanced at him. "You are a most subtle man. You have been guiding my thoughts in another direction, have you not?" She turned the car into the driveway and stopped before the entrance of the double garage. "I am always afraid to drive into it," she explained shyly. "I have scraped the fenders so many times that I leave it to Hiroko."

Masters slid behind the wheel and drove inside. Kimiko was dusting off the chaise lounge when he got out, and he helped her push it into the garden. She made him lie down, covered him with a light blanket, then stole away. He was certain he would remain wide awake until suppertime.

Kimiko's lips on his cheek roused him. The sun had set and the garden was dark. He stretched and drew her down to his chest.

"What time is it?" he asked.

"Almost nine."

"I'd rather stay here and neck than eat."

She chuckled and massaged his shoulders. "We can do both. We will eat then come back out here." His eyes closed under the soothing movements of her hands on his chest. She worked quietly, kneading the muscles of his neck and arms, and when he was about to fall asleep again, she kissed him and drew him to his feet.

At supper, Hiroko was a different girl, almost like a sensible, obedient daughter or friend. She paid no heed to the obvious warmth between Masters and her mother, and even pretended to accept it as an accomplished fact. But Masters kept his guard up, knowing that every statement and action was being stored away for the inevitable showdown. He made no effort to accept the confrontation in the street as the end of her weird actions. Ten years ago, he admitted wryly, he would have waded through a couple of hells for a girl like her. He grinned to himself. Ten years ago, my eye! He would have done it a week ago. He leveled some rice into his mouth to keep from laughing at the thought that he might have done so if she had followed him to the hotel.

Whenever his blood started racing at the thought of the girl, he would turn to look at Kimiko, and immediately a flood of contentment would replace the gnawing desire. He wondered what it would be like when they finally came together. It was sure to happen. It was as definite as anything could be.

His thoughts turned to the time he and Kimiko would live together, probably in this house - with Hiroko. He always like to shave in the nude, directly before taking a shower. The door would open - and Hiroko...

Christ, how could a man live in the same house, knowing that in each dark corner lurked the booby trap that could explode and change everything in an instant.

Or, while he was resting and Kimiko was at the store, Hiroko would take time off from work and crawl into his bed, naked.

He was suddenly aware of her eyes on him, a gleam burning deep inside. You son-of-a-bitch, he reasoned, amused. You know exactly what is going on in my mind. No wonder you could challenge me directly on the street, then sit across from me like a vestal virgin. Also that I have to fight to keep my loins from boiling over just looking at you. Then he chuckled to himself, for he suddenly felt a new surge of strength, an actual desire for combat with this incredible girl.

"What are you smiling at?" asked Kimiko, also smiling.

Masters came back to reality. "Who, me?" His mind groped for a way to explain his thoughts to Hiroko in a way she could not fail to understand. "I saw a little fellow urinating in an alley this afternoon." The incident was so prevalent in Japan that Kimiko raised a brow, as if he said that a car had passed on the street. Hiroko's eyes narrowed. She knew there was more to come. "It reminded me of a game we used to play when I was a kid. To see who could pee the furthest. We would toe a line, then let ourselves go. There was one fellow who was shy about exposing himself, so right before each game he would go home and use the bathroom. The kids tried like hell to get him to pee with them, but after a while they gave up and didn't force him to play anymore."

He chuckled again, and Kimiko joined in because he seemed so pleased. Hiroko wiped her lips with a napkin and leaned back. A faint smile played over her face, then she let one eyelid drop in a very deliberate wink.

Lester Taube

CHAPTER 7

At noon on Saturday, Masters walked out of the lobby of his hotel and stood by the door to wait for Kimiko. She drove up a few minutes later. It was a hot, sweltry day. He tossed his jacket onto the rear seat of the car and set his shaving gear on the floor.

"How are you today?" he asked as he climbed inside. She had visited Ichiro at the prison yesterday afternoon and had been terribly sad during the evening.

"I am all right," she replied. "Did you eat a good breakfast?"

"Yes. I was up before nine. I don't know what this air is doing to me, but I feel like a million bucks."

"Did you get a nap afterwards?"

He placed a hand on her firm, shapely knee and grinned. "One of these days I'm going to sit in your lap and suckle away like a baby."

She smiled in return. "I would enjoy that." She swung into the traffic and set off westward, then reached into the glove compartment and handed him a pamphlet. "I found a shop that had the information in English about the temple."

He glanced at it, then back to her. "Say, did you bring my shirt along?"

"Yes. All washed, ironed, and packed in my suitcase."

"Did you do it?"

"Yes."

"You shouldn't have bothered."

"But it gave me pleasure to do so."

He opened the pamphlet, looked at it for a few moments, then put it down. "Tell me about it. I'd rather hear you talk."

"It is called the Imtambi, a very old temple, perhaps four hundred years old. People go there to be consoled when they are sad and to give thanks when they are happy."

"Who do you pray to?"

"Our deities. It is a Shinto temple."

"How long will it take to get there?"

"About three hours. We could have gone by train, but I wanted to show you the countryside. It is very beautiful. There are flower nurseries and forests along the way."

"Have you been there often?"

"No, only once. After the war. I waited for two years, then went to pray for Ito."

"And now for Ichiro. That's a lot for a lifetime."

She hesitated a few seconds. "Not just for Ichiro. For us, too."

He turned in his seat and gazed searchingly at her fine profile, sensing the utter calmness that exuded from her. How perfect she was - features and poise like an ivory carving, delicately worked, painstakingly polished - an objet d'art.

"What are you trying to say, Kimiko?"

The tenseness in her shoulders was difficult to discern, for she was always erect in her carriage. "That today I shall be your woman."

He had to lean forward to hear her. He stared at her, wondering for the first time how all this could have started, grown, and swept along to this instant. As if every step along the road he had traveled had been part of a plan ordained long before he had first drawn breath, that he would have ended up at this place, at this time, no matter what course he had taken.

"Please do not stare at me so hard," she asked quietly, her eyes still on the road.

"I can't help it. Now it is I who have the thousand questions to ask."

"I will answer one of them. I spoke to Ichiro yesterday and told him about us. Also, that you were one of the soldiers who were at his father's death."

"Oh no, Kimiko. You shouldn't have."

"I had to. He is the head of the family since his father's death. In our way of life he has the authority of his father. I was very grateful for his understanding."

"Why?"

"He asked me if I loved you. I told him I did not know because I had loved only his father, and that you were not the kind of man his father was, but that in your own way you were a man I could be very fond of." A tear rolled down her cheek. "He told me to listen to my heart. I was very proud of him."

Masters turned towards the window, not to look out, but to hide from her the expression in his eyes. "You should be proud of him," he said, gruffly. "Then he knows I am an American?"

"Yes."

"And he did not object?"

"No. He is so much like his father. He understands now that the murder was a bad thing, and having once accepted that fact, he analyzed his feelings and decided not to dislike or hate anything again without first judging it on its own merits. He does not know any Americans, therefore he will not like or dislike until he has had more experience of them. He spoke this way as if he had a lifetime to live instead of a month."

"Good for him!" said Masters, explosively.

"What do you mean?" asked Kimiko, darting a startled glance at him.

"That he hasn't given up. Yesterday, I would have helped the boy, if I had been able to, because of you - or your husband. To me he was just a nonentity of whom we spoke and who irked me because he brought you so much unhappiness. Today, he has identity, and I like him for having found courage and understanding - with all the strikes against him." He looked at his watch. "How about stopping for a while? I know you haven't eaten since sun-up."

"I packed a lunch. Do you mind?"

"No." He pointed down the road. "There's a place, among those trees."

She slowed down, turned onto a path, and came to a halt about fifty yards in. At once, she lifted out a basket and blanket, and found a level spot for the picnic.

Masters watched her kneel to take out the sandwiches and a thermos jug of tea. "You've got a good-looking pair of knees," he remarked.

He was surprised to see her blush. "Keith," she said softly. "Not before tonight. Please."

"Special rites?"

"Yes. Special rites."

"Purification?"

"No. After you spoke to me in the garden, I knew that my past - life, could be overlooked." Her face became more crimson. "I went through these rites almost twenty-five years ago, when I married Ito."

He reached out a hand and touched her lips with his forefinger. "Alright, Kimiko."

When they had finished eating, she made him lie down to rest, then she lay down beside him, snuggling into his arms. Soon he closed his eyes and sank smoothly into slumber, never questioning why his loins did not ache from her nearness nor why he felt more content than he had ever been in his life.

An hour later, she woke him, poured small cups of tea, and soon they were back on the road. It was shortly before five o'clock when they reached the huge park which housed the Imtambi. They left the car in a guarded lot and started up the long trail. It was high in the mountain, the air fresh and strong with the scent of pine needles and well-tended forests.

Every few minutes, Kimiko stopped to make a remark about the temple.

"Come on," smiled Masters. "Don't keep stopping on my account. I've never felt better in my life."

"And I intend to keep you that way," she said, persisting with the pauses, although he was not even breathing hard.

They walked a mile before the temple came into view. It stood in a wide clearing on top of a rounded knoll, a tall, square edifice of hand-hewn stone, gray with the passage of years, like a mountain farmer from the north, shapeless, just a pile of rock with an irregular doorway. In front of the temple was an arch of long, pine logs, peeled and weathered by the sun and the winds, standing guard over this mass of stone dug up from a quarry near the coast and dragged by man and beast to this spot, to make the land holy.

Along one side of the temple stood vase after vase of flowers, impeccably arranged and enhancing the natural beauty of the park, but, in truth, clashing with the grotesque heap of stones rather than paying homage to it. On each side of the path leading to the doorway were small flower stands.

Kimiko purchased two vases of flowers, and, dropping to her knees, rearranged them to suit her taste. Then, handing one to Masters, she led him to side of the building and set hers down against the wall. He placed his vase next to hers and followed her into the temple.

It was a huge vault, dark and damp, oppressive from the fumes of hundreds of candles standing on rough boards along the walls. About three quarters of the distance to the far end stood a wooden railing holding a gate in the center, separating the main room from the sanctuary. To the right of the gate was an upright board with a paper pinned on a cross slat, naming the deities present in the shrine. Two tall candles burned on each side.

Kimiko passed through the gate, washed her hands in a stone fountain, rinsed her mouth, then walked slowly to the altar, bowing and softly clapping her hands.

Masters waited patiently, watching her offer her prayers and place a donation in a metal box. Then she came back through the gate, purchased two candles from a stall near the railing, and handed one to Masters. They lit their candles from those flickering by the gate and placed them on one of the boards at the side of the temple.

Kimiko walked to the center of the vault and made a slow turn, as if she was counting the candles along the walls, then returned to the railing. She folded her hands, bowed, and prayed again.

Masters remained behind, staring intently at her. How small she was, seemingly lost in the vast space of the massive stone temple. Then, before his very eyes, she seemed to grow, to fill the room and rise up to the square ceiling, to press against the bulky rock sides until he felt that they would give way before her. And in his mind, a thunderous bell began to peal.

I love you, Kimiko, his silent cry rang out, and he heard its echo lift off the sides and rebound from the roof and pour through the small doorway. I love you, Kimiko, it rang and rang, and pounded back into his ears until he could hear nothing else, and it filled his brain so that he could not call it out again until the reverberations had died down and this declaration of love had been forever engraved within his heart.

Then she stood erect and turned to look at him - and he understood why this was a hall of God.

She came to him, walking firm and straight, until she was but a breath away - and she bowed. Then he understood even more; that this was the giving of herself to him, that every moment of her life had been carefully saved for this instant, that all the beauty of body and mind and soul had been painstakingly garnered and sheltered and nourished, so that here and now she might offer it to this middle-aged man with the cropped brown hair and light blue eyes and defective heart. Even the memory of Ito.

And for Ito, he returned her bow.

Side by side, they moved to the doorway, and there he stopped to allow her to pass out first, then he turned and looked across the dimness to the alter - and bowed.

When he came out into the sunlight, he stood for a moment to allow his eyes to become adjusted to the glare. She was standing on the path looking back at him.

"Wait here," he said, and went past her to one of the stands. There he purchased a vase of flowers and placed it on the ground next to theirs.

They started back to the car. Halfway down, she stopped and told him to rest.

"What was the third vase for?" she asked.

"Your husband. I owe him a debt."

For a moment he thought she would cry. Then she reached up, took off her jade earrings, and handed them to Masters.

"I marry you," she said simply.

He did not understand the ritual, but instinct took over. He searched in his pockets, and in the end he took off his gold and onyx tie pin with the initial M in the center. He handed it to her.

"I marry you," he answered.

Then side by side, they continued on their way.

At the parking lot, she called over the guard and asked a question. He replied, gesturing with his hand to point out directions. Back on the main road, she continued on for a few miles then turned back into the forest. The dirt road climbed higher and higher until, near the top, it brought into view a large, many-gabled hotel of pine-wood, encircled by a rich, green lawn. Behind the hotel, the mountain fell away into a deep valley, then sloped upward again to a lower, tree covered mountain. Down in the valley, still colored by the setting sun, was a narrow ribbon of water, becoming less and less distinct as the sun's rays filtered and were trapped by the dark forest.

An attendant came out for the suitcase and shaving bag, and they walked up to the registration desk. He wrote 'Mr. and Mrs. K. Masters' on the card. Kimiko made a comment to the desk clerk, and the attendant led them up a flight of stairs to a room overlooking the valley.

When he left, Kimiko opened the windows and drew Masters out onto the balcony. "The temple is there," she said, pointing north.

Below, in the rear garden, was a large fish pond surrounded by wrought-iron tables and chairs. Waiters were placing cloths, silver and glasses on the tables, while others were lighting hooded Japanese lanterns strung throughout the dining area. He put his arm around her shoulders and they stood quietly watching the final red-purple of the sun sink below the mountain line.

"Are you hungry?" asked Kimiko.

"Unfortunately, yes." He looked back into the room. "Where's the bed?"

"We will sleep on mats. The chambermaid will arrange them when we go down to eat."

He chuckled. "Is that the best they can do on my honeymoon?"

"I asked for them. At home, I shall buy a big American bed for you."

"What do you use?"

"A mat."

"Is it large enough for two?"

"No. It is always single."

"Forget the bed. I'm a lifetime away from them anyhow." He reached for her, but she slipped away.

"Not yet, my dear," she said, her eyes twinkling.

He groaned. "More ritual?"

"Yes."

"How the hell do you Japanese find time to have children?"

Laughing, she placed her arms around his neck and stretched up to kiss his lips. "Dear Keith," she said. "I have not laughed like this for a very long time." She took his hand. "Come, we will go to supper now."

They had turtle soup, boiled trout, fresh from the stream, with mixed vegetables and thick, white radishes, melons for dessert, and finally, fragrant tea. Masters leaned back and heaved a sigh of contentment.

He pulled out the package of cigarettes he had bought in the restaurant with Hiroko, lit one, smoked half, then snuffed out the butt.

Kimiko insisted that they take a walk, so they sauntered along the garden paths and into the forest where hanging lanterns lighted the way, then back to the hotel and up to their room.

Kimiko opened her suitcase and took out a long, silk bathrobe. She handed it to Masters. It was powder blue, with a dragon's head exquisitely embroidered over the left breast pocket. In the center of the dragon's head were the initials, KM. She handed him a towel.

"Undress now," she said.

Then turning away from him, she quickly shed her own clothes, wrapped a sheet around herself, and slipped into a silk kimono, free of embroidery, of the same powder blue as Masters. He had already stripped and had wrapped the towel around his waist. Kimiko look dismayed when he put on the robe.

"It is too small in the shoulders," she almost wailed.

"It's all right," he replied. "It would have fitted better when I first came to Japan, but with all this eating…"

She gave him a pair of sandals and slipped a tiny pair on her own dainty feet. Then catching up two large towels, she led him down the hallway to a bathing chamber.

It was a small room, completely tiled on the floor, walls and ceiling, with a showerhead and faucets at one side. Below the shower taps was a second set of hot and cold water faucets and a low, wooden stool. At the far corner was a sunken tub, about four feet square.

Kimiko placed Masters' robe on a hook by the door, then took off her kimono and hung it alongside his.

"Sit, dear Keith," she told him, moving the stool closer to the lower faucets. She picked up a small, bronze bowl and poured warm water over his body until he was completely wet, then soaped a hand cloth and started washing his head, neck, shoulders, chest, arms. At intervals, she laid down the cloth to massage him, kneading the muscles, then rinsed away the soap by emptying bowls of water over him.

He sat there, mesmerized by the touch of her strong, yet gentle hands. She missed nothing, his ears, eyelids, fingers, nails. She washed him, massaged him, rinsed him - then washed him a second time.

She came around the stool and kneeled in front of him, bathing his legs and feet. Then she slid her hand under the dripping towel around his waist and began to soap his hips and stomach.

He looked down at her. Her eyes were fixed on the floor and a calmness was written on her face. He tensed as her hand passed over his loins and he tried desperately to control his muscles. It was impossible. She continued washing him, attempting to appear unaware of the affect of her touch upon him. Tenderly, with great care, she cleansed him - and in her hand was the touch of love.

She rinsed him thoroughly, then finally raised her eyes. "Now you must go into the pool," she said, leading him to the sunken bathtub. There she removed the towel from around his waist and placed it on a hook on the wall.

Masters slid into the warm water and stretched out his legs. The water came halfway to his chest. He leaned back and turned his head to watch Kimiko.

She returned to the faucets, and, with her back to him, loosened the sheet around her, draped it like a mantle over her shoulders, and washed herself. Then she came back to the pool, took off the sheet which had concealed her throughout, and hung it alongside Master's towel.

He gazed, fascinated, at her body. Her slender appearance had been deceptive; she had a firm, full build, with rounded thighs and flat stomach, small breasts, half-mooned and proudly high, and straight legs which tapered delicately into tiny, perfectly-shaped feet.

Like a maiden, she placed one hand over her breasts and the other over the soft hair of her womanhood and joined him in the tub. The water covered her shoulders.

Then she took her hands from her body and held them out to him. He drew her in and kissed her fiercely, her legs rising to encircle his hips as she strained against him, her arms tight around his neck, her lips pressed to his with all her strength.

His hand slipped down to her slender waist, and he pulled her in even closer, and gently, without further guidance, he began to enter her. She trembled in his arms and her lips melted under his. Her fingers bored into his shoulders, and she shifted ever so slightly, feeling for him, closing around him, bringing him deeper within her.

Then she drew away, panting, her breasts swelling and her paps growing large and dark. "Come," she whispered hoarsely. She leaned back against the other side of the tub, and turned him round, drawing his shoulders against her breasts, placing her legs around him. His head rested on the curve of her throat, and lightly, she caressed his chest and stomach, pressing her lips to his ear and cheek.

He felt the raging desire recede and the tension leave his body. An overwhelming peace enveloped him as he lay relaxed in the water, and time stood still - like in the garden when the moment of before was the moment of now, intermingled, fused, as if for the first time in his life there was no need to think.

He opened his eyes. "You are a magnificently beautiful woman," he said.

She hugged him. "I am so glad, my dear Keith. I want to look beautiful for you."

He chuckled. "I never suspected you had so much hidden away in that little body of yours." He could sense the smile in her face pressed to his cheek. His hand played idly with the water. "I remember when one of my fellow officers in Korea came back from rest and recuperation leave and told us what happened when he pulled the plug out of one of these tubs."

She laughed. "Did the owner of the hotel become angry?"

"Angry? The fellow said he almost had a fit. He ran round the room holding his head in his hands and actually crying."

She was still laughing. "No wonder. The tub is just to relax in. The water is rarely changed as it has a closed circulating system. It must have taken an hour to refill."

"The fellow found that out. He had to pay three hundred yen for damages."

She kissed his cheek. "Come, my Keith." They rose to their feet and got out. She placed a heavy bath towel around herself, then, taking up the second towel, she wiped him thoroughly and helped him don the silk robe. Then she dried herself, turning away from him to drop the towel and slip into her kimono.

Their wooden sandals clacked as they walked back to their room. Two mats and headrests were laid out on the floor, side by side. Spotless white sheets and light quilts were folded neatly at the feet.

Kimiko took the robe from Masters, and when he lay down, she covered him with a sheet and quilt, then opened the door to the balcony so that the cool night air and the pale rays of the moon could enter. She turned off the small light. He peered at her dim form as she took off her kimono and hung it next to his robe, then came to her mat and lay down.

He lifted his covers and reached out to draw her onto his mat. She came swiftly into his arms and they lay locked together, feeling the heat in their bodies grow. She stretched upward and pressed her lips to his, and he felt her begin to quiver. She kissed him hungrily and drew away so she could breathe, then searched again for his lips. His hand slid down her back and over her hips, and her trembling increased. He turned her onto her back and kissed her breasts and they swelled even more. A small, low sound escaped her lips. Her hand reached for his shaft with a tentative, exploring touch, and when his fingers passed over the smoothness of her thigh and down to the softness and wetness which waited below, she let out a gentle cry and pulled him on top of her.

They met with an impact that brought deep sighs at the same moment, and they clung together, motionless, for the space of a long breath, heads spinning with the absolute knowledge that each would fulfill the other.

She stirred under him, groping. He pressed in deeper, searching. She wrapped her arms and legs around him, drawing him even tighter, feeling his strength and desire driving within her. Drowned in their urgent need of each other, Masters and Kimiko coupled in breathtaking ecstasy.

Their moment of simultaneous flooding was a predestined climax, for their oneness had been recognized from the start. They came surely and effortlessly, as if each had known there was no need to seek a sign from the other. They came slowly, and it built up in intensity, not bursting the flood gates, but flowing over smoothly, both conscious of the acute pleasure of giving and taking.

They lay still, Masters with his lips against her cheek, breathing evenly, realizing to his surprise that, although his loins were empty and the heat had fled his body, he felt strong and fresh and rested.

Kimiko was also breathing evenly, and her mind dwelt on the same incredible sensation. She felt even more - she felt deep within her the hot flow of the man, and she tightened all her muscles, praying that it might permeate her very system - as he had begun to fill her heart.

Hours later, in the stillness of the night, she awoke. She opened her eyes and found him sitting cross-legged on his mat looking at her. Immediately her mind flashed back to the night in her parents' hut and her waiting by his side. "What is it?" she whispered.

"I was just counting the ways I love you," he said.

She reached up and drew him down to her. They lay together, not speaking, then she caressed his flat-muscled stomach and firm hips, feeling his desire awaken and grow.

She gently turned him onto his back and covered him with her body, making love to him, tenderly, glorying in their mutual need of each other, and bringing forth the overwhelming flooding - as if their union was being continued rather than renewed.

They slept, Kimiko covering him with her light, soft body, still joined together, so that in the morning he need not search for her, but just lift his head to kiss her lips.

Lester Taube

CHAPTER 8

Just before entering the outskirts of Tokyo the following evening, Kimiko turned down the car radio and glanced at Masters. "We will stop by your hotel and pick up your clothing."

"I don't mind staying there. It will be a bit of a shock for Hiroko to have me move in lock, stock and barrel."

"What is this lock, stock and barrel?"

"Moving into your house completely."

"Hiroko will understand."

"After us knowing each other a bit over a week? I doubt it. She may understand our feelings for each other, and perhaps our making love, but moving into your house suggests a rather permanent interpretation of the situation."

"Oh, Keith," she said, lamely. "I never thought you might not feel as I do. Please forgive me."

"Pull over," he said. When the car had stopped, he took her in his arms. "Listen, Kimiko, back there near the temple I gave you my tie-pin." His eyes twinkled. "I'd be lost without it. I have to protect my interest." He kissed her warmly. "I don't know whether that oath we took is legal or not, but I meant it more than if we had signed a dozen certificates and had as many ministers drone it over our heads. I want to live with you, permanently, but I am just wondering if maybe we should do this less suddenly."

"Oh, Keith," she said, smiling broadly. She kissed him heartily. "I am such a stupid woman."

"Easy there. You are talking about the girl I married."

She started the car again and continued on their way. "You will move in, my dear. Hiroko must understand or she will have to accept it without understanding."

"How about the rest of your world? Your friends, neighbors?"

She answered in her direct manner. "You are now my world, Keith."

"That Admiral Kowasachi didn't eye me like I was part of anyone's world. Who is he anyway?"

"He is a gentleman I met three years ago. He wanted to purchase some stock I owned in a trucking company. Since then, he has been cultivating a friendship."

"Maybe he is interested in more than just a friendship."

"Admiral Kowasachi?" She shook her head. "I am not from his..." she searched for a word..."type of acquaintances."

"I am not speaking of marriage."

She said nothing, just concentrated on the road.

"How about it?" he persisted.

"He has suggested a form of relationship." She was clearly uncomfortable.

"What happened?"

"Nothing. I did not expect him to go that far."

"He's a rather imposing person. I would think you would be complimented."

She turned to him. "Keith, the day before I met you, I did not want to become involved in anything but my children and businesses. Something happened to me when you came to my house. Perhaps it is because you are the continuation of Ito. I felt him flowing back into my very being, regardless how you were part of his death. Then I realized even more - that you are a very wonderful person. You touched my heart. I do not believe anyone else could have done that."

She had revealed herself more than was her nature, and it embarrassed her. A thought suddenly struck her. "Keith, I never thought of asking. Do you want to live in Japan?"

He paused to consider it. "I don't know, Kimiko. I haven't really thought of it before. I do know that I want to live with you, and I guess one place is as good as the next. I didn't come here expecting to stay, but I do like it." He shook his head. "I'd better start learning Japanese if I'm going to stay around."

"You do not mind our way of life?"

"If you're speaking of last night, I sure don't," he said, grinning. "I like the food, the atmosphere, the hustle-bustle without becoming nervous. I guess I like everything I've seen so far. But I just can't sit around all day. I'll have to find something to do."

"Are you permitted to work?"

"The doctor said I could, if it wasn't physically too taxing or exciting. Frankly, I haven't the least idea of what I could do here."

"Does just resting bore you?"

"Not so far, but sooner or later I'll have to do something or turn into a vegetable."

"Then why do you not take a course in Japanese while you are resting? Later on, you can decide what you would like to do."

He kissed the side of her throat and slipped his hand under her jacket, fondling a breast. "Still babying me?"

"I enjoy that," she said smiling. "Especially after last night and today."

He took his hand away reluctantly when they entered the heavy city traffic. At the hotel, she came up to his room and helped him pack. He paid the bill, and they started off for her house. When they arrived, she got out, and he slipped behind the wheel to park the car in the garage. Kimiko and the old woman came out to bring in the suitcase and shaving kit. "Scoot," growled Masters, carrying them into the house. "Where do they go?"

Kimiko led him to a room at the rear, which he could see was hers. It was large, brightly papered with scenes of the countryside. Her bedding was rolled against one wall with a handsome chest of drawers and a matching vanity along the others. Low tables, holding vases of flowers, were placed round the room, and a small altar stood in a corner. Sliding doors opened into the garden.

He put down the cases. "I'll unpack," said Kimiko. "Please go to the garden and lie down."

"I should have carried you over the threshold," he quipped.

She came to him and placed her arms around his neck. He smiled at how small she actually was, for she came just above his chin, and he was not a tall man. She kissed him. "Go, rest now, the trip was tiring."

He stretched out on the chaise lounge, and before long he sensed the approach of Hiroko. He opened his eyes. She drew up a stool and sat down. "Congratulations," she said dryly.

"Thanks. You can call me Papa if you want."

She suddenly grinned. "I can't do that. I would be committing incest later on."

He had to laugh. "Didn't you get the moral about the little boy who couldn't pee with his friends?"

"Sure. But he had to pee some time. I'll wait. You're on your honeymoon now, but sooner or later you'll begin thinking how it would be with me. You'll want to see what I'm like in bed."

"When I do, I'll run home to mother and get it out of my system."

"Go right ahead. But one of these nights, while you're making love to her, you'll wish I was there instead. I can wait. Haven't you heard of the Oriental patience?"

"Haven't you heard of the American crack in the face?"

She raised her breasts so they would be more obvious. "I liked it when you struck me in the street. It made me want you all the more."

"It's called masochism."

"I call it a good, healthy, sexual lust."

In spite of himself, he had to laugh. "You shouldn't talk like that to your weary father. Also, you're not supposed to know about those things. How in the hell will I be able to marry you off if all the boys know how lustful you are?"

"They'd stand in line. So will you."

"I'm a happily married man. Go peddle your business elsewhere."

"Nope, I'm saving it for you. But I promise not to seduce you. However, I'm adding a codicil. If mother doesn't remain the happiest woman I ever saw, then I promise to make you pay for it after we're living together."

"How come you're so concerned with her well-being? It hasn't bothered you up to now?"

"I love her, Keith. Don't get the wrong idea about that. I just don't think you're right for her. But I do know that you and I are perfectly matched. If I didn't believe that, I'd back you two up, no matter how much I wanted you."

"You're so damned full of contradictions that you give me a headache. How do you expect your mother and me to make a go of it with you hovering around ready to stick in the knife anytime you can?"

"Come off it, Keith. The day you reach out for me is the day you admit that mother is not the woman for you. If I can take you away, then almost any other good-looking girl could do the same. But if you get by me, then I know mother is safe. Furthermore, I want you badly. That's killing two birds with one stone. If she has to find out, it would be better that she does so before she's an old woman."

He sighed and shook his head. "Man, you give my headache a headache. Why don't you be a good daughter and help your mother in the kitchen?"

"Are you tired? Want me to rub your back?"

"Like hell I do. The next goddamn thing you'll have my pants off."

"See!" she chuckled. "You're thinking about it already."

They heard Kimiko coming out. She drew up another stool and sat down with them. "It is getting dark," she observed, "but it is too nice to put on the lights." She looked anxiously at Masters. "Did Hiroko say anything?"

"Yes. She decided to call me Papa."

The girl laughed. "I'm glad you brought him home, Mother. I haven't heard as much laughter here for a long time."

"I am glad you have accepted it so well, Hiroko," said Kimiko, visibly relieved. "We were very much concerned."

Hiroko rose. "I'm going downtown to get a sandwich and take in a movie."

"Eat supper here," suggested Kimiko.

"Not on your life." she called out cheerily, starting off. "You're on your honeymoon. I sure wouldn't want you along on mine."

After they ate supper, they went for a stroll in the garden. "It is good for you to take a walk after meals," said Kimiko. "The book says so."

He tightened his arm around her shoulders. "Does the book also tell you what a wonderful person you are?"

She liked that. She led him into the house and made him lie down on the sofa and place his head in her lap. Slowly she stroked his hair, and time drifted by as they relaxed and listened to light music from the radio.

When they entered the bedroom, she stopped and turned to him. "I knew this before, Keith," she said softly, "and was more certain when I gave you my earrings and became your wife last night. I love you."

He did not remind her that it was the first time she had said those words, nor did he reveal how desperately he had longed to hear them. Instead, he reached out, swept her up in his arms, and carried her to their sleeping mats.

On Tuesday afternoon, Masters accompanied Kimiko and Hiroko to Mr. Takahashi's office. The attorney greeted them formally while an assistant bustled around the room arranging chairs. He spoke slowly so that Hiroko could interpret.

"I spent the morning with the Minister," he said, "and his decision is that the sentence must be carried out as ordered."

Kimiko blinked and made an effort to keep from crying out. It was impossible: a hiss of pain broke from her lips. Hiroko's eyes filled and she swallowed several times before she could go on.

"I do not see what further action can be taken," continued the lawyer. "I am afraid that we must bow to the inevitable. Ichiro, however, has been considering a confession of his guilt. I assume this is his way of making peace with his conscience. It would certainly not alter the sentence, and would, in fact, result in more adverse public opinion. He has requested that I ask you if he should remain silent or confess."

"My son must make the decision," said Kimiko.

The lawyer nodded. "I said as much to him, but he insisted that I ask his mother, for a confession would bring more shame on his house."

Kimiko's face remained expressionless. "My son must make the decision," she repeated.

Masters sighed and stood up. "Mr. Takahashi, will you please carry a message to Ichiro from me?" The lawyer nodded. "Then tell him," continued Masters, "to remain silent. We will understand." He looked down at Kimiko. "Okay?"

She stared straight ahead, looking into space, then turned her eyes to the lawyer. "Please give Ichiro the message. It is from me also."

They left the attorney's office and drove home together in silence. Kimiko went directly to her room, and Masters knew she was going to pray in front of the small altar in the corner of the bedroom.

"Come outside," he said to Hiroko, and led the way into the garden. "Sit down," he ordered. She sat immediately, alerted by his tone. He eyed her closely. "Hiroko, they are going to execute Ichiro and there isn't a damn thing that can be done about it." He paused. "Unless we take the law into our own hands," he stated softly, flatly.

She leaned forward, excited. "You mean to help him escape?"

"Keep your voice down," he growled. He took out his package of cigarettes and lit one, relishing the bitter taste in his mouth. "I can't think of anybody in this world whom I'd rather not discuss this with than you, but I need help and you're the only one I can turn to. Now, can you get time off work - for a vacation?"

"Yes, I can take time off whenever you want."

He looked at his watch; it was shortly before four o'clock. "Go to your office right away and put in your request. Try to get three weeks at least."

"All right, Keith." She stood up to leave.

"Wait a minute," he called. He stood for a few seconds thinking. "Get some maps of the west coast of Japan and of - "his brow wrinkled, "Hong Kong, China, North Korea and Siberia."

"All right, Keith," she replied quietly, subdued.

"Now, get."

When she had gone, he went to the bedroom door and called Kimiko. She came out wearily, her eyes red from weeping. "I'm going downtown, Kimiko. I may not be back until late. Do you mind if I leave you now?"

She shook her head, unable to speak.

He left the house and walked until he found a roving taxi, then directed the driver to take him to the United States Army Headquarters. It was almost 5 p.m. when he arrived. It was a large administration building, and directly inside the lobby was a military police desk. A sergeant was seated behind it.

"Sergeant, I'm an ex-soldier from World War Two and Korea, and am now on a visit here. Do you have an officers' directory? I'd like to see if any of my friends are back over here."

"No, sir. But we have a telephone book that's unclassified." He handed it over. "You'll have to look at it here, though. We're not supposed to let it out."

"Why not?"

"There's just so many, and headquarters had a gang of complaints about salesmen swiping them and bothering the people."

Masters looked round and saw a table to one side. "May I look at it over there?"

"Okay, sir."

He took it to the table, sat down, and studied the lists. Captains of fifteen years ago, he reflected, would be lieutenant colonels now. Just for the hell of it, he looked at full colonels also.

He found the names of two or three officers that rang a bell in his memory, and jotted them down. Then his finger stopped and his heart skipped a beat. "Jesus Christ," he said aloud. Lieutenant Colonel W.C. Wilson, Headquarters, Operations.

He took the phone book to the desk sergeant. "Sergeant, how can I find out the serial number of this officer?" The MP eyed him. Masters grinned. "If he's the one I think he is, his serial number is very close to mine. We were at OCS together." He wrote his own number on a pad and handed it over.

"Okay, sir." He put in a call to the officers' records section, spoke briefly, then put down the phone. "He's your man, sir."

"Thanks." Masters copied Wilson's office number and his home address. "Will he still be in?"

"I doubt it. They generally leave at a quarter to five, but I'll give it a try." He made the call. "He's already gone, sir."

"Could you ring his quarters for me, please."

The MP was cooperative. He dialed and handed the phone to Masters. It rang, then a woman answered. "Hello."

"Hello. My name is Keith Masters. I'm a friend of Colonel Wilson. Is he home, please."

"One moment." He heard her call out, "Honey."

Wilson almost jumped through the phone. "Keith, is that you?"

"Hi, Bill. Still shacking up with strange women?"

"That's my wife, you wild bastard. Where the hell are you?"

"I'm at headquarters. Seems that I just missed you."

"You stay right there. I'll be over in ten minutes, driving a blue Buick. Anyone with you?"

"I'm alone."

"Freeze in place," he ordered, then said something like "Goddammit," and hung up.

Masters walked outside and leaned against the building, thinking hard. The honk of a horn brought him out of his reverie. Wilson was waiting at the curb and had opened the door for him.

They shook hands, excited as boys. "Jesus Christ," said Wilson. "I almost flipped when Betty said Keith Masters wanted to talk to me." He eyed the smaller man. "You haven't changed one iota. Put on a few more pounds, though." Wilson was a tall, slim man with blond hair, dressed in sports jacket and slacks.

Master smiled. "Time hasn't changed you very much, either. What is it - fourteen years?"

The tall man sobered. "I ought to know. Yeah, fourteen years." He edged the car into the traffic. "What are you doing in Japan? Back in service?"

"No. I had a bit of heart trouble last year. Just loafing around. Got the bug up my ass to see the old haunts."

Wilson turned an anxious eye on him. "Nothing serious, I hope."

"No, I'm okay. Just not supposed to climb hills anymore. Got your family over, eh?"

"Yes. Betty and the kids will be tickled to see you. I've talked so much of you over the years that they'll never believe a meek-looking shrimp like you was the wild bastard I spoke of. What gives with you and the domestic stuff?"

"It didn't work out. We were divorced."

Soon they arrived at a large apartment complex and parked in a lot. A sign stuck in the grass directly in front of the vehicle read: LT. COL. W.C. WILSON.

"Brass hat, eh?" remarked Masters.

Wilson laughed. "Anyone over sergeant gets the same sign."

His apartment was a plush, field-grade officer's quarters, four bedrooms, two baths, modern kitchen, handsomely furnished with quartermaster items, supplemented by personal pieces collected during tours around the world. Betty Wilson was a tall, plain, bright-eyed woman of forty or so, from Montana, and Bill proudly introduced his son, aged sixteen, and a daughter of ten. He took a picture of a boy about nineteen years old from the mantelpiece. "My oldest. Name's Bob. He's going to UCLA, but is spending the summer with my folks in New Jersey."

The daughter opened the conversation. "Sir," she asked politely, trying not to dance around. "Are you the one who saved daddy's life when he was shot?"

"Well," said Masters, pretending to think hard. "If I remember correctly, your daddy was still going pretty strong. I had to pull him out of the fight because he was so mad."

"That's not the story we heard..." started Betty. A wink from Masters cut her off. She began mixing drinks, and when Bill told her about Master's heart, she made him a glass of lemonade while she and Bill took scotch and water.

"Where are you staying?" asked Bill.

Master lowered a brow in warning. He and Bill had met twenty four years before at officers' training school, had soldiered together for a while in World War II, and then the rough year in Korea. He did not have to draw a picture for Wilson. "At a friend's house," he answered, glancing at the children.

They chatted until supper, and after they had eaten, the boy and girl left while Masters, Bill and Betty settled down in the living room.

"What's up, Keith?" asked Bill.

"I'm staying with a Japanese woman. We'll get married when I can find out how it's done over here."

There was no visible reaction, except for Betty saying, "Let's all get together some evening," or something to that effect, and hurriedly leaving the room to supervise the Japanese maid taking care of the dishes.

Bill grinned. "It shakes the round-eyed women to hear about those cute babies nabbing the hometown boys."

They gabbed and reminisced, and after a while Masters got down to business. "Bill, I've decided to take up writing. Had a couple of articles accepted by a magazine a while back, and thought I'd take a shot at writing a book."

"Christ, write an autobiography. That would make good reading."

"It would have to stop after Korea. There wasn't much to it after then. Anyhow, I'd like to write an adventure story with an army background. When you have some time, I'd appreciate being brought up to date."

"How about now?" he asked. "Do you need classified stuff?"

"I doubt it, but if I ask about anything which is confidential, you just lower the boom."

"Okay." He began to outline the new ROAD organization of the army divisions, and got a pad and pencil to explain their structure. Masters waited patiently, putting in a question here and there to throw him off the track.

An hour passed swiftly, and Master decided it was time to probe for the information he sought. "Bill, the plot is about an American officer in Japan. He's a major, so he can still be young enough to screw around." They grinned at each other. "The major falls for a Jap doll." His eyes twinkled. "I'm catching up on that part now." Bill chuckled. "Anyhow, the doll is a real bitch - will screw anything that walks, and is head over heels in love with this Jap who is a spy for the Commies. She helps him by conning the major into turning over secret files. To give the story color, I intend to bring in the intelligence people, the Jap cops, and just about every group, including the Boy Scouts.

"The major is no dummy, but he is really hung up on this girl." Masters' mind turned to Hiroko. He could see how a nice, solid guy from St. Paul, for example, would take secret files for her. "Although the plot has been used a couple of million times, I believe the background color will make it different."

He leaned forward. "Bill, who would handle this kind of case?"

"Hell, that's basic. The counterintelligence."

"Would the Jap police come into the picture?"

"Well, generally we'd try to handle it ourselves, but you must remember that we have a Status-of-Forces agreement now which subjects all Americans to Nip

law. We could take care of the major if he was on a
military installation, but if he was on Nip property, like
in his gal's bedroom, we'd have to get the Nips to
knock down the door, or tap phones, or stuff like that."

"With which section of the Jap government would
the counterintelligence work?"

"The National Police. They're actually a
paramilitary organization, and could be turned into an
army overnight."

"Do they have a counterintelligence section?"

"Damned if I know. I guess so, but it would be
hidden under another title, like the Political Science
Board, or some shit like that. I'll get the poop for you
if it isn't classified."

"Thanks. One more question. Suppose this major
walks up to a cop on the beat and asks him to help him
apprehend an American soldier. Would he do so?"

Bill scratched his head. "Wow." He thought for a
while. "If the soldier was doing anything contrary to
Nip law, the cop would arrest him without being asked.
But if not, it would be a toss-up. He could help or
refuse. If he had a feather up his ass about Americans,
and officers in particular, he could say that he would
have to first check with headquarters."

Masters interrupted. "But suppose the major said
there was no time?"

"Then it's the old army buck-buck game, Keith.
The cop would have to make the decision as to whether
he wants his ass chewed for failing to use his initiative
or have his ass chewed for acting without an okay from

his headquarters. One thing is certain, though. If he told the major to go to hell, he'd really be in hot water."

"What's you personal opinion?"

"Well, the Nips are probably the most intelligent people I've come across. You don't have to draw them a big picture before they catch on. If the major had a valid reason and explained it properly, I think the cop would give him a hand. But if the major permitted him to have one shred of doubt, he would bow and scrape and be as courteous as hell, but stall until doomsday to check it out first."

That was it. Masters made a bit more polite conversation, then looked at his watch and said he would have to go. Bill would not hear of him taking a taxi, so Masters fobbed him off with a story that he was meeting his shack-up-girl at his old hotel, so Bill grinned and let him off in front of it.

"Keith," he said, and he was serious. "Don't let us lose contact again." He felt somewhat bashful at asking the question. "How are you fixed for money?" Then before Masters could answer, he continued, "I've been sorta flush these past few years and I'd like to help."

"Thanks, Bill. I'm okay, but I promise to ask if I need some help." He watched the taillights of Bill's Buick being swallowed up in the traffic, and thought with fondness of the tall, blond, lieutenant colonel. Then he hailed a taxi and went to Kimiko's. He was not about to let Wilson know that he was living with the mother of a boy scheduled to be executed for murder.

CHAPTER 9

It was nearly midnight when he got home, but Kimiko and Hiroko were waiting up for him. Kimiko was worried at the lateness of the hour, and breathed a sigh of relief when the taxi drew up and he got out. She hurried down the pathway and looked at him anxiously. "Are you all right?" and before he could answer, she went on, "I didn't know whether you took your pills with you. I forgot to ask."

He smiled and hugged her. "In my pocket, darling."

She straightened at the word, 'darling', as if each time he said it, it was like saying 'I love you' a dozen times. "Are you hungry?" she asked, when they got inside.

"No, but I could use a cup of tea." She rushed to the kitchen. Masters motioned with his head to Hiroko and they sat in a corner. "Did you get your leave? "he asked softly. She nodded. "How about the maps?"

"In my room."

"Okay, I'll get them tomorrow. Does your mother know you are taking leave?"

"I didn't know whether you wanted me to say anything so I haven't told her yet."

He almost smiled at her. "Good, don't say anything." He remembered that Kimiko and Hiroko drove downtown together each morning for work. "Take the maps with you tomorrow and meet me at ten o'clock at my old hotel."

"Okay."

After they drank their tea, they went to bed. Masters understood the heaviness of Kimiko's heart after the meeting with the lawyer, so he took her in his arms and comforted her with a kiss, then gently rocked her until she fell into a restless slumber. He remained awake long after, thinking hard. The shell of an idea had already formed in his mind, but so much was speculation that its outline was obscure. Dawn was breaking before he also fell asleep.

At ten the following morning, Hiroko was waiting in front of the hotel. Masters eyed her sternly. "Let's get one thing straight," he stated brusquely. "No screwing around."

"All right, Keith. I think I know what you're after, so I declare a real truce for the time being."

"Another thing," he continued. "You may know what's going on, but I don't want you involved. Get that clear in your mind or you can go back to work and tell them to cancel your leave."

She didn't scare easily. "No dice. It concerns Ichiro. I'll take my chances the same as you."

"Then beat it."

"Stop it, Keith. You need me and I can handle my own end. But I'll do whatever you say. I want to help."

His face creased into a smile and he tapped her beautiful jaw lightly with a fist. "Okay, so long as you do exactly what you're told, no more and no less." He stepped closer to her and lowered his voice. "Listen, Hiroko, I don't quite know what we're going to do, but whatever happens, you've got to understand one point - and remember it every second; once a plan is made, you've got to follow it to the letter - or it falls apart. Looking around the doorway when you're told to stand stiff and quiet can be the little thing that ruins everything. Do you get that?"

"Keith," she answered steadily. "If you tell me to sit in front of a train, I'll stay there until you say move or it runs over me."

He pressed her arm. "Good. Now let's go in and get a room. I bet the clerk is getting dizzy with all you women coming up and waiting in the lobby and cars and stuff. I bet he'll figure your mother has already thrown me out."

"I'll tell him that mother sent us back here for me to teach you the facts of life."

"Christ, can't you ever get your mind off that?"

"You started it, not me."

The clerk thought exactly what Masters said he would. He eyed Hiroko wistfully, leaning over the counter to watch her walk up the steps with Masters. Masters was given a different room from the one he had had before, and it was just as small. Hiroko immediately kicked off her shoes, sat cross-legged on the bed, and drew out the maps. He caught on, took off his shoes, and joined her.

They were good maps. Masters suddenly snapped his fingers. "Hiroko, go to Mr. Takahashi's office and find out which countries do not have extradition treaties with Japan. Phrase it coyly. But if you can think of any other way of finding out, do so. Don't mention your name, though. Your brother may still be remembered."

She was off the bed, shoes on her feet, and out of the room in a flash. When the door closed behind her, Masters admitted to himself that he was glad to have her helping him - she would be a valuable accomplice.

By noon she was back. "The public library has a legal section," she explained, "and a list of countries with treaties, effective nineteen fifty-four. I charmed the fellow at the counter. He's a law student and says there have been no changes." She looked squarely at Masters "He also tried to date me, but I told him I was meeting my lover."

"Did you tell him your lover was not in a screwing mood?"

"He wouldn't have believed it. He looked down the front of my dress when I leaned over. You should look too, then you'd understand."

Masters shook his head and chuckled. They studied the list of countries together. "There's none with North Korea," she pointed out. "They don't like us Japanese, but they know we're the smartest in Asia. Also they don't like the U.S., and they know we're friends."

He had already decided on North Korea while she was away, if it did not have an extradition treaty with Japan. He had felt that the odds were against them having one. It was hard to make the next decision, but it had to be made. "Okay, Hiroko, you've hit the spot. Now look over the west coastline." He pointed out a town. "Go there, visit the neighboring villages and find a boat to hire which can travel..." he studied the map more closely, "at least five hundred miles. It must not carry a crew of more than two or three men. Say that you want to rent the boat for a fishing trip for your father and brother." He suddenly stopped. "Shit," he said. "You can't go. They'll identify you afterwards."

Her head rose. "I don't care."

"What did I tell you about obeying orders?" he snapped. "Do as you're told and shut up. We're not planning a tea party. Somebody could get killed."

Her face paled. "All right, Keith."

He thought quietly for a few minutes. "Do you know where the American Army Post Exchange is?"

"No, but I'll find out."

"Check it over, see who goes in and out, whether they're in uniform, who inspects identification, everything."

"Okay."

"Then visit the jail where Ichiro is kept. Make a drawing of everything you can find out, where he is kept, where the guards are stationed, when they change, how he eats, all the details you can think of. But above all, keep as low a profile as possible." He eyed her beautiful face. "Can't you make yourself less noticeable? Mess yourself up, flatten those tits you're throwing around, wear cheap clothing."

"All right, Keith, I'll be careful."

"Just a little over three weeks. Christ, there isn't much time. Let's go."

He left her at the front of the hotel and took a taxi to Kimiko's building. She brightened when he entered the office, but sobered immediately at the serious expression on his face. Inside, he wasted no time. "Kimiko, I need your help."

She felt alarmed but quickly regained control. "In what way, Keith?"

"I need two things. First, that you trust me implicitly and don't ask questions. They will all be answered in time."

She nodded. "I will trust you."

"Second, I need money."

"How much?"

"The equivalent of ten thousand dollars. Do you have it, or even a part of it?"

She didn't bat an eye. "Do you want cash?"

"Yes."

"Do you have time to eat first? It's after noon."

"No, I don't have time. Another thing. I will be leaving for a few days."

She could not prevent shock and uncertainty from showing in her face. She tightened her lips. "All right, Keith, we'll go to the bank now. It's just around the corner."

He could not remember a time when he wanted to take her in his arms more than he did at that instant. He stood quietly while she took a bankbook out of a locked drawer of her desk and slipped on her jacket. Without speaking, they left the store, walked down a block and around the corner to a large, modern bank. An official immediately came over and greeted her with a politeness denoting deep respect. Within minutes, she placed a thick bundle of notes in her handbag and they walked out into the street. In silence, she handed the money to him.

She was a proud person, but transcending the pride was her womanliness. "Do you want me to pack for you?" she asked.

"No," he said, and leaned forward to kiss her, ignoring the fact that it was not the custom to kiss on the street in Japan. She raised her lips to meet his. Then she turned and walked stiffly back towards her office.

He caught the first taxi he could find, returned to the house, ordered the driver to wait, then hurriedly packed his bag, slipped a small Japanese-English dictionary into his pocket, and rushed back out. "The railroad station," he said.

At the station, he learned that all his rushing was for nothing: the train to the west coast did not leave for another two hours.

Friday evening was another lonely night for Kimiko. She sat with Hiroko, watching television, but the programs could not hold her interest. She rose frequently to walk in the garden, then to her room to look again at the few articles Masters had left behind. She went into the kitchen and ran a cloth over the spotless sink and stove and refrigerator that the old servant had cleaned thoroughly just an hour before. She decided to polish her nails, went into the bedroom, sat in front of her vanity, and arranged the bottles. Then she placed them back into the drawer and returned to the garden, sitting on a stool near the chaise lounge.

She was sitting there when she heard a car drive up and stop. Her heart began to pound and she gripped the seat of the stool, waiting with bated breath, imagining the opening of the car door, the paying of the taxi driver, the unlocking of the gate into the front yard, the short walk to the door, the searching for the key, the placing of the key in the lock.

Then she heard his voice and was able to breath again. She hesitated no longer but rushed into the living room and into his arms, leaning her head against his chest, hoping he could not hear the terrible hammering inside her.

"I'm hungry," he said and it was the most beautiful command she had ever heard.

Later in the night, she took the tired man in her arms, rocking him as he had once rocked her, and when he turned on his side to sleep, she took off her night dress and snuggled up to his back, molding her body so that she could get as close to him as possible. In his sleep, he reached out for her arm and drew it around him, holding it tightly. Then she went to sleep."

Masters met Hiroko in the hotel at ten the following morning. "How did you get these?" he asked wonderingly, when he saw the detailed drawings of the prison and the list of interior information.

She was very proud of herself. "I went to the city architect's office and told them I was writing a thesis for my economics work and wanted to check on housing. It took me a day to work my way to the plans of the prison, and I could make only brief sketches. Then yesterday I went to the prison itself and asked to see Ichiro. They refused, as it wasn't visiting day, so I got lost a few times and wandered around. The police were very polite and helpful - they didn't want me to go." She was tempted to explain why they wanted her to stay around, but decided not to harass Masters at that time. He should be able to see why.

He studied the drawings. "My God, it's like a fortress."

Hiroko's slim finger pointed to one side. "If you could get over this part of the wall and out through the bars of this window, you would be inside Ichiro's cellblock."

"What are the cells like?"

"A guard said that each cell holds from four to ten prisoners. There are fifteen to twenty cells in a cellblock, then a steel door and a passage, then another steel door and the next cellblock." She opened her purse and took out a pencil and pad to make a swift sketch.

"Where do the passageways go?" asked Masters.

"I don't know. I imagine they lead to the offices."

He shook his head. "It would take a commando raid to break it open." He looked again at her neat drawing. "How do you know that getting through this window will put you in Ichiro's cellblock?"

"One of the guards insisted on showing me the way out, then tried to date me when we got outside. He pointed to the right-hand side of the prison and said that Ichiro's cell was there - on the second floor."

"It would never work," he said. "First, the outer wall must be scaled, then I'd have to cross twenty feet to the prison and up to the wall." He took out the package of cigarettes, lit one, and felt his head swimming as he inhaled the raw smoke.

"You shouldn't smoke," said Hiroko.

"All right." He put out the cigarette. "What about the Post Exchange?"

"There's a woman at the doorway who looks at cards the people have to show her."

"ID cards," explained Masters.

"What are they?"

"Identification cards, containing the person's picture and fingerprints. Were the men in uniform?"

"Some of them were. But most of them were in civilian clothes."

"Are there any military police at the door?"

"Now and then one would come up and stand around a while, then he'd go away. There are none posted at the entrance."

He patted her shoulder. "Well done, Hiroko, you did a good job."

She straightened on the bed as if he had given her a present. "How did you make out?"

He hesitated, then took out his wallet and handed her a folded sheet of paper. "Copy this," he said. "It's the name of a boat owner, the location of his boat, and all the details for the escape. If anything happens to me, use it as you see fit." He glanced at her, self-consciously. "I'm going to spend a great deal of money for expenses. Your mother gave me ten thousand dollars which should see it through. I hope it works - that's a lot of money to take chances with."

She chuckled. "I can see you're not a gigolo. Mother is pretty wealthy, she won't miss the money." Hiroko eyed him with a sparkle in her eyes. "Don't ever underestimate mother. She's a sharp businesswoman and a lot more intelligent than she seems. Besides the stores, she has property and companies all over town."

"You're kidding."

"Not in the least. She gave me fifty thousand dollars in stock when I became twenty one."

Masters laughed wryly. "What's that for?" asked Hiroko.

"I was going to insist that she take a hundred and fifty dollars per month from me for expenses. I can't live off anyone, least of all a woman."

"She would like you for it." She paused a moment. "Just how are you financially?"

"You've got exactly fifty thousand dollars more than I. I get three hundred dollars a month disability pension."

She placed her hand on his. "I didn't know things were that close for you, Keith. Can I help?"

He patted her hand. "You're not such a bad kid when you stop fooling around. No, I've got all I need. But I didn't expect to start playing house with a wealthy woman. I figured that she was comfortably off, and that we'd both pitch in to make ends meet. I'm not the kind of person who can tell whether a sofa costs twenty bucks or two hundred dollars."

A frown creased her brow. "Is it going to make any difference? About the money?"

"Hell no. Your mother doesn't put on a big front, and as long as it stays like that, I don't mind. But now it will make me a little uncomfortable to have her tear all over the house to serve me a cup of tea when I know she can buy and sell me all day long."

"Maybe that makes her happier than buying big houses and cars," said Hiroko, softly.

"You're getting out of character, acting like a true daughter."

She shook her head. "I'll remind you again, I'd do anything if I knew it would help her. I still just don't think you're the right one for her."

He rose and stretched. "Christ, talking to you is like riding on a merry-go-round." He thought of something. "Get me the names and addresses of a few car rental agencies in town, and all the newspaper articles about the killing of that union man and subsequent trials."

She was out of the room in a second. He stood looking at the closed door, a smile on his face. Then the smile faded, and he took a deep breath. For a moment it reminded him of the deep breath he used to take before charging into the face of the enemy.

CHAPTER 10

The officers' housing area was dimly lit. Masters sat in his rented Toyo Crown sedan and glanced at his watch; it was almost 10 p.m. Across the way from him was an apartment house containing six apartments, two on each floor, and bolted to the front of the building was a row of mail boxes with the names and ranks of the occupants. Most of the tenants were Lieutenant Colonels.

He sat quietly until he saw the headlights of a car approach the parking area. At once, he slid out of his car, entered the main door of the apartment house, and went up one flight of stairs. He stood there listening. When he heard the vehicle pass the parking area and continue on, he slowly walked down the staircase and back to his car.

A second car drove towards the area half an hour later, and he got out and repeated his movements. Soon he heard the sounds of several people entering the building. Immediately he started down the staircase. It was a family of five. "Good evening," he greeted them, then continued on his way back to the car.

His next alert was also a family, and again he repeated his greeting and resumed his post.

At midnight, he gave up and drove back to Kimiko's house.

The following night he selected a second apartment complex that also housed Lieutenant Colonels, and again it was fruitless.

He chose still another for the next night, and took up his vigil at 10 p.m. A few minutes after arriving, he saw headlights approaching, and walked to his position on the first floor. The lower door opened and the sound of a man mounting the staircase came to his ears. At once, Masters started down the steps, coming upon a man about his own age. "Good evening," he said.

As the man replied and passed him, Masters whipped out a stubby piece of lead pipe and struck!

The man let out a low moan and sagged to the steps. Masters grabbed the body to break its fall, then ran trembling hands through the pockets. There was a wallet, some coins, car and house keys, personal papers. He pocketed them, then felt the man's pulse - it was beating steadily. He hesitated a moment, then reached down and took off the wristwatch.

Quickly descending to the doorway, Masters stepped into his car, started it, and drove out of the parking area. At the main street, he switched on the headlights and raced out of the housing section, then slowed down and drove steadily to Kimiko's. He parked the car around the corner to conceal it from her.

Inside the house, he went directly to the bathroom, locked the door, and took out the wallet. He had struck well - in it was the identification card of Lieutenant Colonel Charles Durkin. He sighed as he replaced the wallet in a pocket, then went to the dining room to have a cup of tea.

Hiroko had done her shopping early. By the time Masters arrived at the hotel the following morning, she had already secured half a dozen plasticized cards and a package of razor blades. It took very little time for him to learn that they could not scrape off the plastic from the test cards without causing irreparable damage to the cards themselves, and he therefore realized that he could not change the picture on Durkin's ID card.

"Damn," he grunted. "Well, I'll just have to take a chance." He opened Colonel Durkin's wallet to the first tab, which contained the ID card, and slipped in a small photo of himself to cover the Colonel's picture. He closed the wallet and snapped it open again. It looked pretty good as the tab held the picture firmly in place.

"Suppose they ask you to take the card out of the wallet?" asked Hiroko.

"Then I start running," said Masters, dryly. He handed her two photos of himself. "Go to Yokohama and use that charm of yours to have the name Charles Durkin printed on my picture. Look closely at the size of the lettering on Durkin's photo, and make sure they're the same on mine."

"Okay," she said, and, characteristically, sped out of the room.

At supper, she waited for a moment to be alone with him and said, "Tomorrow."

Saturday afternoon was a cloudy, humid one. Masters walked through the outer doors of the Army Post Exchange, strode up to the young Japanese girl seated behind the identification stand, then pulled out his wallet and flipped it open towards her.

"Afternoon," he said.

She glanced at the picture, saw the likeness, and nodded. "Good afternoon, sir." Masters walked into the PX.

He purchased an officer's green uniform for $48, a field officer's cap for $19, poplin shirt, black tie, black shoes, belt, socks, Lieutenant Colonel's leaves, a number of decoration ribbons, a combat infantryman's badge with star, and, after a moment's deliberation, General Staff Officers' insignia.

At the hotel, it took half an hour to affix the ribbons and brass to the jacket, then he put on the uniform and looked at himself in the mirror. It was a good fit.

It made him feel taller and more powerful, but it also made him feel a little ashamed, as if he were disgracing it. He changed back to his street clothes, packed the uniform in his suitcase, and went down to the desk. The clerk glanced at the bag. "Keep my room for me," said Masters paying him two weeks' rent in advance. "I'll be visiting a little, and coming back from time to time." The clerk smiled and bowed.

He drove to a larger hotel, registered under his own name, and in the room he put on the uniform. Then, as a Lieutenant Colonel, General Staff, he went downstairs and into the street. He walked around for an hour, ill at ease in his false attire, returning the salutes of officers and soldiers he met from time to time. The lesser ranks called out a cheery "Good afternoon, sir", and when he met a full Colonel, he saluted and said, "Good afternoon, sir", and the Colonel saluted, nodding his head in reply.

Masters returned to his room, mussed up the bed and the bathroom, then donned his civilian clothes and drove to Kimiko's.

For the next four days he followed a strict routine. At ten each morning, he met Hiroko at the small hotel to discuss plans, at eleven he was at the new hotel where he changed into uniform and walked the streets. At three in the afternoon he returned to disarrange the bed and bathroom, and at eight in the evening he left in civilian clothes to return home.

He hoped his movements were sly enough to allay any possible suspicions of the hotel employees. It also gave him the opportunity of breaking in the uniform and feeling more at ease in it.

Throughout all this, Kimiko was unbelievably patient, not asking a single question or attempting to find out what was happening. It was obvious that Masters was up to something, for his disappearances during the daytime were brought to her attention by the servant, who was promptly rewarded with a sharp rebuke. His nonappearances at the store for lunch were a similar wrench at her heart, and his arrival home after eight-thirty each evening was an added factor to her uncertainty. But she said nothing, suppressed all questions inside her, and fought with them when they reared up to tear at her mind.

She also sensed the unease of the man in the night. He was as tender and fulfilling as he had been the night of their first union, and although both of them had withdrawn part of themselves into secret alcoves, they brought physical contentment to each other by their eager desire to give instead of receive. But he was restless in his sleep.

Masters in turn, felt a remorse which weighed heavily upon him. Often he was tempted to tell Kimiko the facts, for he was aware of the battering their relationship was taking. But he held back, for he could not bring himself to involve her in the criminal action being planned, nor subject her to the false hopes which had such little chance of being realized.

Then one morning, when he met Hiroko in the small hotel room, he eyed her closely. "Friday," he said simply.

She sat cross-legged on the bed and looked at him. "Will whatever you are planning to do be dangerous?"

His laugh was a sharp bark. "Are you kidding?"

She took a deep breath. "Is there any risk of you being killed?"

He shrugged. "There could be. If a guy hid from everything which could kill him, he'd have to keep off the streets and out of bath tubs."

"I'm calling off the truce, Keith," she stated quietly.

"For Christ's sake, Hiroko, I've got enough on my mind without you fooling around again. Leave everything alone until this is over. I may not even get to first base on this try."

She shook her head. "Stop arguing for a minute, Keith, and listen to me carefully. We've gone over all there is to discuss about you and mother and me. But this is something else. I want you to make love to me before Friday. And I hope I have your child because of it."

His face darkened and she could see the rage building up. She held out her hand, imploringly, and he controlled his temper. "I want us to make love for ourselves this time. I've come here morning after morning, and every time I've climbed the stairs and opened the door and walked into this room, I've felt my stomach turn over from wanting you so badly. I want you to be with me once - just one time. Then no matter what happens, whether you're killed or die or live forever with mother, I can remember that I've had the touch of you.

"Keith, please, it's not some foolish thing I'm asking of you. It's truly important to me. You've probably had enough women in your life to fill a room. What's so important about one more girl, especially if it means so much to her?"

He stared at her and understanding came into his eyes. He leaned forward and kissed her. She clung to him, and slowly they sank down on the bed. She pressed her body against his and he felt the fire building up inside her. He forced himself to draw his lips away, then rested his face upon her cheek. "Can you hear me, Hiroko?" he asked.

Her body stilled its movements against him. "Yes, Keith."

"Then listen to me and try to understand me as I've finally understood you. I've wanted you from the first moment I saw you, and a couple of dozen times since, and even more so right here and now. If I sound like some goddamn virgin afraid of getting into trouble, it must be because there is a really important reason. When I told you the first time you came to this hotel that your mother was my last chance, I don't think you understood.

"A little over a year ago I almost died. I had almost died a number of times before then, but this was the first time I couldn't fight back. It gave me a chance to take the first frank look at forty-five years of living - or what I called living. In my thoughts were a string of bars and women and wild times. They all added up to zero. Even a son who hated the thought of me. I also thought of your father."

He felt her tense. "I took out the picture and the card I brought your mother, and I looked at them over and over again, and somehow I felt even more certain that every year of my life had been wasted - and that I had wasted a helluva lot of other, innocent people's lives. If my ex-wife hadn't hated me beyond all hope, or if my son didn't despise me as much, I am convinced that I would have started working like a son-of-a-bitch right then and there to make things a little more right for them. In all these crummy forty-five years, I hadn't accumulated one friend I could turn to - to give a little bit of myself. The picture of your father and mother, and you and Ichiro, was my last chance to try to win back something from all those years. Maybe I was seeking atonement, an expiation for all this waste."

He drew back his head so he could look at her. She was lying open-eyed, listening closely. "I don't know why I came to Japan, or what I intended to do when I got here. A Japanese teacher in Chicago told me that your name was that of a peasant, and in the back of my mind I pictured you people as backwoods farmers without enough money to live on. I thought that giving you part of my three hundred dollars each month would ease the loss I felt, would dispel the desperate fear of dying without having once done something good for someone.

"It didn't work out that way. After seeing your house and learning that your mother owned those stores, I realized that the few bucks I could give were unnecessary. Then I eyed your mother, and right away the forty-five years of absolute rottenness came back out. I decided to give her a little bedroom joy to carry her over the hump of being without a man for twenty years. And, believe me, I also considered the idea of pushing you down on a bed if the opportunity presented itself. Maybe it was chagrin. I don't know. But I do know that I had decided to play around and then hit the trail.

"Your mother took me to your grandparents, and on the way back I became aware of the fact that perhaps I could help. It made me feel like an ex-drunkard who was about to take a shot again, suddenly finding a more important reason not to drink any more. It restored my determination to make amends.

"Then, when we visited the temple, I got the shock of my life; I found myself in love with your mother. I had been a little bit in love with her before, like the guy who is going to sleep with a strange woman and kids himself into believing it's going to be a big deal, but at the temple I fell absolutely in love, and I knew that if I could prove how I felt, I could die ten minutes afterwards and that everything would not have been wasted.

"Ichiro is my second hope. I wouldn't give two bits for the chance of success, nor for me still being alive after the effort. But I've got to go to the wire or I am guilty of waste again.

"Now you, Hiroko, whom I love as a woman. It would be the easiest thing in the world to take you from here, to run far away and enjoy the wonderful days I could have with you. But then, I would be wasting everything again - your mother, Ichiro, even you. Our few months or years together would reopen the wounds, because I would still be taking, always taking, not giving.

"Then there's the most important thing. I want your mother's love more than I want you, or Ichiro's life, or even my own."

He stopped talking and turned on his back - and he suddenly knew he had finally reached the point which gave meaning to his crummy forty-five years.

Hiroko lay quietly beside him, then raised her head to rest it on his shoulder, and her arm went around him. Idly she stroked his chest, his throat and cheek. Suddenly she rose to her knees and kissed him. "All right, Keith," she said. "You and mother, you can both count on me." Then she was off the bed, had slipped into her shoes and was out of the room.

Masters watched her leave. She's made it, he thought. She's made it all the way. That makes two,

Kimiko and her. He got up from the bed, feeling the weariness deep inside him, and his mind turned towards the third one. Today was Wednesday; there wasn't very much time.

Masters phoned Colonel Bill Wilson at his office from the second hotel. "Hello, Bill," he said. "Got a few minutes?"

"Hi, Keith. Thought you would ring me before now. When are we getting together again?"

"I've been working like a madman on that book. Almost have the title picked out for it."

Bill chuckled. "I get the first copy, hear?"

"Okay. The trouble is that I may have to join the goddamn army to find out what's going on these days. Bill, this is a nutty question, but what the hell is this FASCOM jazz?"

"That's the new Field Army Support Command. They've taken most of the combat service support units, supply, transportation, medics, and a gang of others, and lumped them under a new headquarters. It's supposed to tighten jurisdictional control, leave the combat troops unburdened to do the fighting, and make support more efficient. No more moon-light requisitioning - you get what you should without having to trade underwear for paint."

"Do you have the breakdown of the command and staff?"

"Yeah, it's around somewhere. I'll look it up and have it for you in an hour or so."

Masters spoke very distinctly. "I have to dash off in a few minutes. My shack-up girl is taking me to the boondocks for a couple of days. I'll be back Friday afternoon, between one and three." His voice became more casual. "Will you be at your office?"

"Sure, I'm a working man."

"Bill, I'm working on the chapter which takes in some of that FASCOM jazz, so if you would please have it ready when I call Friday, I'd be much obliged. The trouble is that I'll be leaving again right afterwards. Are you sure you'll be there?"

"Boy, you writers. All you do is dash off for pussy, get a couple of facts, then off again for pussy. Yeah, I'll make a point of being here, no matter what."

"Thanks, Bill. I'll arrange that we get together next week."

"Okay. Hey, she got a friend?"

"What size and color?"

"Anything who doesn't resemble my wife."

"You mean anyone. Didn't they teach you English in the army?"

"I mean anything, you wild bastard. Let me know what you can dig up."

"Okay. So long."

There was still one more thing to be done, and it turned out to be the most difficult so far. In his Colonel's uniform he visited three sporting goods shops and attempted to purchase two handguns. It was a shock to learn he would require a police permit. In desperation he turned to pawnshops, with even less success, for none of them dealt with handguns. One pawnshop owner suggested that he check out gunsmiths, and after an afternoon of rushing frantically from place to place by taxi, he found exactly what he wanted - two slender pistols at three times their value, but with no strings attached. He bought a box of cartridges, and back in his hotel room he familiarized himself with the guns, then locked them away in his suitcase.

At supper, Hiroko brought up the last part of the plan.

"Mother," she said. "I'm taking off work for a few days. A couple of the girls in the office want to go to the mountains, and asked if I could drive them. May I use the car?"

"Of course," Kimiko replied, glad that the girl could divert her mind from the relentlessly approaching date that faced Ichiro. "When do you want to go?"

"Tomorrow, right after breakfast."

Kimiko nodded in agreement, then turned to Masters. "There is an old Japanese show on television Saturday night," she said shyly. "Would you like to see it with me?"

"Sure," he replied quickly.

Kimiko paused. "It begins early though, at seven-thirty."

He understood her hesitation, for he always arrived home later. "Okay," he said. He brought the bowl of rice to his lips and levered some in with the sticks to hide the wistful expression which he feared might show on his face.

CHAPTER 11

Hiroko was a few minutes late the following morning. He could hear her trotting up the staircase to his room in the hotel. "Sorry," she said, as he held the door open for her to enter. "I had trouble finding a parking place."

"Do you have the pictures?" asked Masters.

"Yes, and they're very good." She handed him an envelope. Masters opened it and spread a number of photos upon the bed. He leaned over to study them. Hiroko, as usual, slipped out of her shoes and stepped on the bed to look from the opposite side.

"These are the best," she said, pointing at two of them.

"Yes, they're excellent. You've gotten some good shots."

"I was there all afternoon before I got exactly what you wanted."

Masters picked up the two photos she had indicated. The first was of a slim American soldier coming out of the Post Exchange. By his side was a Japanese girl carrying a paper bag. The second photo was a blow-up of the soldier's face. Both pictures were slightly fuzzy, as if the range setting had not been properly adjusted, but they would be clear enough to someone who knew the people well. Masters studied several photos of other soldiers with Japanese girls coming out of the PX, and concluded that the ones chosen by Hiroko were the best.

"I'll use these," he said, placing the two pictures in his pocket. He handed the remainder to her. "Destroy them as soon as you can." He looked at her trim figure dressed in a light, wool dress. "Where are your gloves?"

"In my purse. Want to see them?"

"No, I'll take your word for it. Are you ready to go?"

"Yes."

They walked out of the hotel and got into Kimiko's Datsun, then she drove him to a nearby car rental agency. In half-an-hour he came out in a small Nissan. Hiroko was waiting a block away, and led him through the city to the highway traversing the island to the west coast. They drove steadily in separate cars for a couple of hours, then slowed down and turned off the road into a woods. Hiroko took out a hamper of food and prepared a picnic among the trees.

"Are you going to stay in Japan afterwards?" she asked him.

Masters stopped chewing the chicken sandwich. "If I'm still alive, and can get a job." He knew that he was just making conversation.

"What do you want to work for? Mother has plenty of money."

"May have to send a daughter of mine to school to learn how to speak respectfully to her father," he said, chuckling.

"No kidding, Keith. We know you didn't come after mother for her money. She's got enough for both of you. Why worry about it?"

"Just a strange American custom. Anyhow, I'd like to work again. It doesn't have to be much, just work that is interesting."

"What can you do?"

"Not a helluva lot. I opened an appliance shop right after the war, World War Two, that is. Went broke so fast that I think it was a record in the city. Then I peddled vacuum cleaners, door to door. Got the surprise of my life when I made more than I spent. Then Uncle Sam tapped my shoulder and told me to straighten up the Korean mess. Afterwards, I sold life insurance. Know anybody who needs a guy with all these high class talents?"

"There's a lot of things you could do here."

"Name one."

"I don't know offhand, but I bet I could find a few as soon as I put my mind to it." Masters grinned, he was absolutely sure she could. Hiroko could do anything she wanted to, and do it well. "Want me to put my mind to it?" she asked, seriously.

"Yes, you do that, Hiroko, you do that. Come on, let's get going."

They continued driving, stopping only for gas, and at mid-afternoon Masters took over the lead. He could smell the sea as he entered Takada, a few miles from a small fishing village on the coast called Naoetsu. He slowed down at a central parking area, signaled for her to stop there, then drove on a block and waited. She parked Kimiko's car, locked it, and joined him quickly.

Masters made a U-turn and started back. "Put on your gloves right away," he said.

She flushed. "Sorry," and reached into her purse to take out soft driving gloves.

He handed her a handkerchief. "Here, wipe the door handle, inside and outside. I've told you a dozen times to listen to orders."

"Sorry, Keith. I'll pay more attention."

"You'd better, or you'll foul everything up."

It was evening by the time they returned to Tokyo. Masters stopped the small Nissan and turned to her. "Where are you staying?"

"I have a room in a motel about ten miles from Yokohama."

"You'll have to take a taxi there. I don't want to be seen with you."

"I understand."

"Where are the duplicate keys to the Toyo?"

"Here." She opened her handbag and dangled them before his eyes.

"Now don't forget, you must not touch those keys or the car without wearing gloves. Not with one little pinky, understand?"

She nodded, still smarting from the incident at Takada.

He held out his hand and a tight smile crossed his face. "You'll do well, Hiroko, I know you will. I couldn't have gotten to first base without you."

She took his hand but wasn't able to smile back at him. Instead, she leaned forward and kissed him full on the lips. "Can I see you again, tomorrow morning?"

He shook his head. "No. If anything goes wrong, you just follow my instructions and sit tight."

"It won't go wrong, Keith," she said, with a quaver in her voice. Then she pushed open the door and jumped out. He could see she was close to tears.

He drove the Nissan to the spot he had selected a few days before, parked it on the street and left it unlocked. "Be good, you little bastard," he murmured, with affection.

Nearby was the four-door Toyo. He got in, drove to Kimiko's house, and again parked around the corner. It was almost 10 pm.; he had returned later than planned.

Kimiko was obviously worried, but her relief at his appearance was even more evident. "Have you eaten, my dear?" she asked.

"No. Would it be too much trouble to scrape something up?"

Immediately she was in the kitchen rattling pots and pans. He followed her inside and leaned against the doorway. "You've got a good looking backside," he remarked, studying it with satisfaction.

She tried to hide the smile, but finally gave up. "I think yours is pretty good looking, too," she replied, keeping her eyes firmly fixed on her cooking.

"Men don't have good looking tails. Only girls do. You especially."

"That's what you men think. I say that yours is beautiful."

"Why don't we introduce them to each other?"

"Before or after you eat?"

"The hell with food."

She turned, and he was struck once more by the amount of love he could see in her eyes. She groped behind her and turned off the stove. The weariness of the long drive fell from his shoulders as he stepped closer to her. "I've got something special to tell you tonight, Kimiko."

"Yes?" she whispered, never taking her eyes from his.

"I love you more than I have ever loved before, and more than I ever thought I could love. And starting tonight, I promise that we'll never be apart, never, so long as we live."

She flung her arms around his neck and he picked her up, marveling again at how light she was in his arms and yet so strong and full underneath. He carried her to their bedroom and laid her gently on the mat, kneeling beside her to look long and searchingly at her, as if to etch her loveliness into every fibre of his being and to give every cell of awareness one more opportunity to record how very dear she was.

Then he stood up and began to remove his clothes.

CHAPTER 12

Keith Masters, alias Lieutenant Colonel Charles Durkin, fully uniformed, with battle ribbons on his chest, got out of the taxi at the main gate of the Tokyo Central Prison. He paid the driver and turned to look at the high, stone building which stretched a block square, then at the narrow guard towers jutting out above its walls.

Heaving a deep sigh, he tightened his grip on a slender attaché case and started up the main entrance steps. A husky Japanese guard came to attention, saluted, then opened the door for Masters to pass through.

Inside, to the left, was an information desk. He strode over to it. "I wish to speak with Captain Watanabe."

The desk guard motioned to a man seated next to him, who rose and came to the window. "Yes, sir?"

"I wish to speak with Captain Watanabe."

"Who is calling, please, sir?"

"Lieutenant Colonel Charles Durkin."

"One moment, please, sir," said the guard, picking up the desk phone. Masters glanced at his watch; it was exactly six minutes after one, on a Friday.

The guard spoke rapidly over the phone, hung up, then came out of the information booth. "Please, sir," he said, motioning to Masters to follow him. He led the way down a corridor, knocked on a door, and stood aside for the American to enter. It was a small office; two women were sitting behind desks, typing, and a slim, middle-aged man was leaning over a filing cabinet.

The middle-aged man straightened and bowed. "One moment, please," he said politely, knocked on a door to one side, and passed through. Soon he returned and held the door open for Masters.

Masters walked into a large, austerely-furnished office. A long, heavy desk stood in the far corner, with half-a-dozen chairs ranged in a semi-circle in front of it. There were no pictures, paintings or ornaments on the walls.

Behind the desk sat a stout Japanese, dressed in a plain guard uniform, a number of decorations pinned to his breast pocket. He was about sixty years old, his grey hair as closely cropped as Master's, a carelessly trimmed, grey, mustache drooping over his upper lip.

The Captain heaved himself out of his chair and bowed. He was not tall, a few inches shorter than his visitor. Masters returned the bow with a courteous nod. The Captain motioned to a chair and Masters sat down.

"Do you speak English, sir?" asked Masters.

"Somewhat," the Japanese replied. His voice was low and full. Masters breathed more easily. "However," he continued, "if the conversation should be one of an involved nature, I respectfully request that I be assisted by one of my aides."

"I have no objection, but the subject is highly confidential."

"Would my adjutant be acceptable?"

"By all means."

The officer pressed a button on his desk, and within seconds a light tap sounded on the door leading to the corridor. He pressed a second button. There was the click of an electric lock and the door opened. A tall, solid man of about thirty years of age entered and bowed to the two seated men.

"My adjutant, Lieutenant Fujii," said Watanabe.

Fujii bowed again to Masters, and sat down at a nod from his chief. Watanabe looked at Masters, waiting.

"I am Lieutenant Colonel Charles Durkin of G-2, Counterintelligence. My identification." He took out his wallet and opened it, leaning forward to show it to the Captain. The officer peered closely at the picture, name and rank. He nodded, and the hammering inside Masters' chest slowed down. Masters turned the wallet towards the adjutant. He is the dangerous one, he reflected.

Fujii's eyes fastened on the identification card. Masters could see him hesitate, as if he were considering reaching out to take the wallet and study it more closely.

"I have," smoothly continued Masters, closing the wallet without haste and placing it back into his pocket, "come to you on a rather delicate mission. This project has heretofore been supervised by one of my assistants, but has reached a point which requires coordination with your office."

Captain Watanabe's unblinking eyes flickered ever so slightly in acknowledgement of the compliment to his position.

Masters opened the attaché case and slid out a folder. "In early nineteen hundred and sixty-four, January the eighth, five men assassinated a Mr. Adachi, a labor union official. One of the murderers was a man named Takaaki Saito. He was executed on February eleventh of this year."

He paused to glance at the two police officers. They nodded. Masters took two photos from the folder. "Have you ever seen this American?" he asked, passing them to Watanabe.

The heavy man peered closely at the photos, then reached into a drawer to take out eyeglasses, slipped them on, and restudied the pictures. Finally he passed them to his adjutant, who scrutinized them more carefully. An almost imperceptible sign passed from Fujii to his Captain. "We have never seen this soldier," said Watanabe. "But if you wish, I can have them relayed to our identification section for further inspection."

"That's quite unnecessary at this stage, Captain," said Masters. "I was almost certain that he would not be known to you, but there was the very slender possibility that he might be. This soldier," Masters tapped the pictures, "has been in Japan for almost three years now, and has been under surveillance since his arrival. We suspect him of being a member of the Communist Party in the United States. Therefore, he was assigned to a nonessential position at headquarters where we could keep him under observation.

"A year ago he married one of your nationals, and five weeks ago we intercepted a telephone call between them. The call originated from our headquarters," he added hastily, to explain that the army was tapping only their own lines. "One remark was of specific interest to us. He said to his wife, "Invite Saito's friend to supper".

"This comment was filed away without any special action being taken until a periodic review of his dossier was made two weeks ago by the officer in charge of the case." Masters gave a slight shrug, as if to explain that, being police officers, they should understand that important matters were sometimes overlooked. Watanabe almost smiled. "The officer immediately decided to investigate the name, and a few days ago he concluded that there might have been a connection between the American soldier and Takaaki Saito."

The Captain and his adjutant were leaning forward with great interest. At this point, Watanabe reached into his desk, took out a package of cigarettes, and offered one to Masters, who refused with thanks. The officer lit one and leaned forward again.

"There are two reasons," continued Masters, "why we must expedite this matter. First, the soldier is scheduled to be rotated to the United States in about fifteen days, and then discharged. From that point on, the case no longer remains a military counterintelligence project but is handed over to our FBI. Second, we have learned that an accomplice of Saito in the murder of Mr. Adachi is still alive and in your custody. His name is," he looked again at the dossier, "Ichiro Tanaka."

The Captain nodded. "Yes, he is scheduled for execution in ten days."

Masters sat back in his chair. "I see," he said, wrinkling his brow in thought. For a few moments there was silence, then Masters leaned forward and placed his elbows on the desk. "Captain, would you please assist me in a test? Would it be possible to have one of your people casually state, so that Tanaka can overhear, that an American soldier, by the name of Corporal Walter Hutchins, was responsible for revealing the identity of Saito to the police as one of the murderers of Mr. Adachi? The comment must be made in such a manner that Tanaka does not realize it was meant for his ears."

Watanabe glanced at Fujii and nodded. The adjutant rose at once. "The name is Corporal Walter Hutchins?" he asked.

"Yes."

"Very good, sir." He left the room.

Masters and the Captain made small talk, and once the officer raised his great bulk from the chair and waddled into the outer office. Masters tensed. When he returned, he was carrying a paper which he placed on his desk. "Excuse me, please," he apologized, and began to read it carefully, then signed it and pressed a button. One of the female secretaries came in and took it.

Masters glanced at his watch; it was eight minutes before two. He fought his growing nervousness by taking out his own pack of cigarettes and offering one to Watanabe. The officer lit them both and they continued to talk idly as they smoked.

At four after two, Fujii returned. "I had two guards take Tanaka from his cell on the pretense of inspecting it. In the waiting room a door was left open, and from the adjoining room I personally made the remark to the cell-block Sergeant about Corporal Hutchins. The two guards later told me that they clearly overheard my comment and were certain that Tanaka did also."

"Excellent," said Masters. He turned to the Captain. "Now sir, I would like to have these two photos shown to Tanaka. He is to be asked if he ever saw this man. Please have his reactions studied."

The officer finally understood, and a flicker of amusement and respect came into his eyes. He nodded to Fujii, and the adjutant promptly left the room.

He was back in a few minutes. "Tanaka says he has never seen this man before. The general opinion is that he is telling the truth."

Masters pursed his lips, seemingly disgusted. "Do your people know him well enough to determine whether or not he is lying?"

"The cell-block guards state that he is a quiet boy who does as he is told and gives no trouble. They have, however, observed his reactions to a number of stays of execution, and insist that he has demonstrated his feelings quite openly."

Masters sighed. He glanced at his watch and pursed his lips again. "Captain," he finally said. "Would you please have a call put in to Lieutenant Colonel C.

Wilson at the United States Army Headquarters? Here is his number."

Watanabe picked up the phone in a huge hand and ordered his secretary to place the call. It came through at once. Masters took the phone. "Hello, Bill, what do you have for me?"

"Oh, hi, you wild bastard. How was the trip?"

"Not too good," he replied carefully, pressing the receiver tightly to his ear. "What have you learned?" he asked, distinctly.

"Wait a minute. Here, I've got it. FASCOM is commanded by a Major General with a BG as assistant FASCOM commander."

"Hmm, that's way up there," he replied, careful not to look at the Captain and his adjutant.

"Well, it's a helluva big organization, so they need a lot of brass. The major sections are..."

Masters cut him off. "Hold it a minute, Bill." He began to grope in his pocket for a pad. The Captain bowed as he pushed over a tablet and pencil. Masters nodded his thanks. "Okay, go ahead," he said to Wilson.

Bill began to give the organizational information, which was not classified. Masters deliberately wrote '3:30 - 4 p.m., corner Yatsushiro-Dori Avenue and Senda-Dori Street'. Underneath, he wrote the name 'Howard Barnes'. He listened until Wilson had finished with the major components and was about to start on the subordinate sections.

"Okay, thanks, Bill," he interrupted. Wilson paused in surprise. "Incidentally," he continued, clearly and distinctly, "that person we spoke of..." he hesitated.

"Who? Oh, the gal. How are you making out?"

"I'll have further information for you a little later today."

Bill's tone abruptly grew quieter. "Hey, Keith, is somebody there standing at your shoulder?"

"Yes."

"Your shack-up?"

"Yes."

"I get it. Okay, give me a buzz when you're free - or do you want me to recite the alphabet to keep her guessing?"

"I'll try to set it up this afternoon," said Masters, and hung up.

He sat staring at the phone, thinking, then ostentatiously raised his arm to look at his wrist watch. He cleared his throat, and glanced up at Watanabe. "Captain, two men will be at this address between three-thirty and four o'clock. One of them will be Hutchins, and the second will be a man we also have under observation. Is it possible to have Tanaka taken there to look them over and tell us if he has ever seen either of them before? The photos I gave you are not very clear." He glanced again at his watch. "There is very little time and this is an extremely important case."

Masters leaned forward, trying to ward off the feeling of danger that the quiet adjutant radiated. "In addition, is it possible to get the prisoner as close to them as possible, perhaps using binoculars to observe?"

Watanabe's eyes turned towards Fujii. Masters struggled to keep his gaze fixed on the stocky man and not turn. Chills began running up and down his spine.

The accordance, when it came, almost upset Masters' iron-willed composure. "Very well," said the Captain, and nodded towards his adjutant.

CHAPTER 13

At exactly twelve minutes before three, Fujii led Masters into the courtyard of the prison where a small, unmarked police car was waiting. On the front seat was the driver, and in the rear was a second officer with a boy seated on his left. They were handcuffed together. The guards were dressed in civilian clothes, and the boy wore an ill-fitting, prisoner's uniform.

Masters glanced at him as he entered the front seat. He was Kimiko's child, there was no question of that. The year and a half in prison had made him pale, his eyes were downcast, his shoulders drooping in dejection, but there was no doubt who he was. Even if he had not seen pictures of the boy at Kimiko's house, Masters would have recognized him. He appeared to be slightly taller than Hiroko, with a more solid bone structure, and in the fine features and the rather long jaw - which were family characteristics - he saw the mother and the sister.

"Are you sure the guards speak English?" asked Masters.

"Yes," said Fujii. He turned to the officers. "Do you have your instructions well in mind?" he asked in English.

"Yes, sir," they said. The one in the back held up a small pair of binoculars. "I have the glasses, sir."

The driver leaned forward to see his chief better. "And I have the correct address - at the intersection of

Yatsushiro-Dori Avenue and Senda Dori Street. We can be there before three-thirty, sir."

Fujii raised a brow at Masters, who smiled back. "Thank you," he said. The adjutant nodded, closed the door of the car, and waved the driver off. He drove slowly through the courtyard to the gate. The gate guard, evidently expecting the vehicle, immediately opened the steel door and allowed it to leave without an inspection.

They turned southeast towards the city center, then swung west into a quieter sector. Masters glanced at his watch; it was 3:15. He swiveled in his seat and faced the guard in the rear. "Does the prisoner know what he is to do?"

"He speaks English, sir," cautioned the guard. "Yes, he knows what he is here for."

Masters looked directly at the boy and his heart thumped at this first actual confrontation. "What are you to do?" he asked him.

Ichiro's eyes remained fixed to his lap. "I am to look at two Americans and to tell you if I have ever seen them before." His English was not as precise as Hiroko's, and was heavily accented.

"Very good," said Masters, turning back in his seat.

"It's directly ahead, "said the driver, motioning with his hand.

"All right," said Masters. "Pull over to the curb." While the vehicle was slowing down, he peered along the lightly-trafficked street for other police cars. There were none. But he was apprehensive, afraid of that prison adjutant and the thoughts which might come into his razor-sharp mind.

The car stopped. Masters and the officers leaned forward to scan the corner, about fifty yards away. There was a restaurant on the near side. "They will meet there," said Masters, pointing it out. "May I have the glasses, please?" The guard in the rear handed them over. Masters focused them on the corner, then slowly swept the area. There were a number of people walking along the sidewalk, and cars passed from time to time. He scrutinized the people lounging about or stopping to look into windows, then turned his attention to the parked cars along the street, searching to see if they contained any police.

When Masters was satisfied that all was normal, he gave back the binoculars, lifted the attaché case onto his lap, and unhooked the snaps.

The driver's attention was on the corner when Masters' hand slid into the case and drew out a pistol. With the same swiveling movement he had used to turn to speak to the rear guard, Masters crashed the weapon against the driver's temple! The man's head snapped back! His eyes widened. Then he fell forward against the steering wheel.

Masters did not pause to see the results of his blow. The pistol swiftly continued its turn and stopped, aimed directly at the officer in the back. "Don't move, or I'll kill you where you sit," he growled.

The guard flinched and his mouth popped open in amazement. "Ichiro!" called Masters. The boy's eyes, rising at Masters' command to the guard, focused on the American officer with a leveled pistol. "Ichiro, you told someone to listen to the heart. Do you know who I mean?"

The boy hesitated, then his eyes narrowed. "Yes."

"I am the one spoken about. Do you understand me? Quickly!"

He was Hiroko's brother, for he grasped it immediately. "Yes," he said, astonishment written on his face.

Masters handed over the second pistol. "Put this in the guard's ribs. If he moves, kill him," he said flatly.

The boy took it gingerly, then squared his jaw and thrust the muzzle into the officer's side.

Masters glanced at the driver; he was still unconscious. He lowered the gun to his lap to conceal it, and quickly scanned the street. All was still calm. He turned back to the guard. "Unlock the handcuffs," he snapped.

The man swallowed, then reached into a pocket and pulled out the keys. In an instant the cuff was off the boy's wrist. "Come here," Masters growled at the officer. The man sat forward, completely unafraid, fury flaming from his eyes. Masters raised the pistol and brought it down savagely on his head. A cotton cap cushioned the blow, but he knew that it had been a good one. The guard slid limply to the floor.

A man and woman paused by the car, looking curiously at them. Masters motioned roughly for them to keep going. The woman grasped the man's arm and pulled him along.

"Come, Ichiro, hurry!" said Masters, jumping out of the car and striding back along the street. In seconds, the boy was at his side, baggy prison uniform standing out like a sore thumb. The small Nissan that Masters had rented was only half a block away. Quickly they leaped inside.

Several people had collected around the police car when he sped by, but he blanked out of his mind the many things which could happen and concentrated only on the route he had prepared so diligently and over which he had driven a number of times to familiarize himself with the turns and traffic.

In fifteen minutes they were through the busy section of the city and speeding along the quieter streets leading westward out of the metropolis. Half an hour later they were on the highway traversing the island. Soon he saw the turn-off he had selected, and slowed to enter the forest. Hidden amongst the trees the Toyo was waiting - and Hiroko.

She was leaning against the rear of the car when they came into view. With a cry of relief, she rushed towards them, pulling open the door before he had completely stopped and throwing her arms around Ichiro.

Masters' eyes flashed to her hands - they were encased in gloves. "Later," he snapped, bringing their attention to him. "Quick, get him in the car!"

Hiroko grasped Ichiro's hand, led him from the small vehicle to the open trunk of the Toyo, and told him to lie down inside. Masters drove the Nissan deep into the woods, turned off the path, and parked it among a clump of bushes to conceal it. He trotted back to the larger car and got down on the floor of the rear seat. "Okay, Hiroko," he called out. "Let's go." They bumped over the rough path, then it became smooth as she turned onto the main, asphalted highway. In minutes she was racing westward.

"Not so fast," Masters growled. She slowed down. He looked at his watch; it was almost 5 p.m. Then, for the first time that afternoon, he listened to his pounding heart, drew in a deep breath, and closed his eyes.

He opened them quickly enough about forty-five minutes later. "Keith," called Hiroko, and he sensed from her tone of voice that it wasn't to ask the time.

"What's up?"

"There is a line of cars ahead. I think the police are checking them."

"Don't slow up yet," he warned. "Keep driving normally. How far ahead?"

"About a quarter of a mile."

"Hiroko, listen closely. Don't panic. Are there any turnoffs?"

"No, Keith." Her voice was shaky. The car slackened speed.

"What are the police doing?"

"They're inspecting the cars. There are a number of Nissans on the side of the road. They're checking them closely."

"Are they looking in the trunks of the other cars?"

"I don't think so." The Toyo was just crawling along now.

"Listen, Hiroko," he said, speaking rapidly. "Do everything you can to distract the inspector, make eyes at him. If he hesitates one second, wave at him, say thank you, and take off - slowly. Do you hear?"

"Yes, Keith."

"If he opens my door, give the car the gas and break out. Then get ready for me to jump up front and take the wheel. Do you hear?"

"Yes, Keith."

"Don't panic, Hiroko, don't panic."

She didn't answer, for she had come to a stop. Masters drew a blanket over himself and lay back, breathing hard. He cursed himself for letting her get involved in this. Then his hand slipped to the pistol in his belt, and he drew it out.

The car moved forward a few feet and stopped again. He could hear a man talking. The voice came closer. Then he heard a man speaking directly beside the car.

Hiroko asked a question and the man replied. She made a remark, and they both began laughing. She added something else - then the car started moving.

He found that he was trembling. After a minute or two, Hiroko called back to him, "It's all right, Keith." Her voice was quavering.

He loosened his grip on the pistol, and threw off the blanket, breathing as if he had run uphill. "What happened?"

"I did what you told me. When he came over, I asked him what was going on, and he said they were looking for two men." Her voice regained confidence.

"I told him to let me know if he found them, because I was in need of a man. He laughed. Then I wished him good hunting and took off. He waved goodbye."

Masters shook his head, chuckling. That Hiroko. The man who gets her should give thanks every morning, noon and night. "Good work," he called out.

It was after eight and growing dark when they reached their first stop. Hiroko pulled into a small woods and shut off the ignition. Masters climbed out, stiff from lying in a cramped position, stretched his aching muscles, then reached for a package wrapped in brown paper which was lying on the rear seat. Ichiro was already out of the trunk, seemingly unaffected by having lain in a ball for three hours. He and Hiroko were talking rapidly in Japanese.

"Here," said Masters, handing him the package. "There are clothes inside. Change." The boy took the bundle and went behind a tree. Masters took another package from off the seat and began stripping off the uniform. Hiroko, unabashed, helped him disrobe and put on his suit. Then she took a food hamper from the front seat and began to lay out sandwiches and cokes.

"Keith," she called. He walked over to her. "Were you afraid, when we stopped?"

"A little."

"I would have panicked if you hadn't spoken to me."

He patted her shoulder gently. "No you wouldn't. You are one helluva person, Hiroko." When Ichiro came up, Masters took a sandwich and a coke. "We have about an hour," he said to them. "So, go ahead and talk, but keep your voices down."

He walked through the darkness towards the main road a hundred yards away. At a position a few yards from the edge of the tree-line, he squatted, placed the pistol by his side, and began to eat. He chewed slowly, stopping the movements of his jaws to listen better whenever a car approached, then continued eating as it sped by.

Towards the end of the hour, he rose, stretched, and returned to the car. Hiroko and Ichiro were seated in the front, talking. He got into the back seat. "We still have a few more minutes. Hiroko, did you take off your gloves to eat?"

"No, Keith, I have done exactly as you told me."

"Did you open your purse or drop any personal effects?"

"No, I didn't wear any jewelry except my watch, and I didn't touch my purse."

"Okay. Did you explain the rest of the plan to Ichiro?"

"Yes."

"How about corresponding later? Have you decided on a system?"

From the silence, he knew they had not. Hiroko began speaking in Japanese, then stopped and switched to English. "Write to father's youngest brother," she told the boy. "And sign your letter with an O."

Ichiro was staring through the darkness at Masters. "I cannot tell you how grateful I am, Mr. Masters."

"All right, but spend the time talking to Hiroko and giving her messages for your mother. We will have time to speak later."

He sat quietly, listening to them, then after a while he sat up "Well, we must get started now."

Ichiro returned to his place in the trunk, Masters resumed his position in the rear of the car, and soon they were back on the highway. Hiroko drove steadily, and just before midnight he heard her call out, "We're almost there." He rose from the floor and saw they were coming into Takada. Lights from a few houses were still burning. She entered the town, drove by the parking area, and stopped a block further on.

"Keith," she said, softly.

"Yes."

"Do we have a few minutes to talk together?"

"No. It is always the few minutes which destroy a plan."

"Where will you really go - afterwards?"

"I don't know. Maybe try for South Korea. Tell your mother to sit tight - I'll write when I'm able to." He reached into his pocket. "I almost forgot, here's four thousand dollars. I've kept out enough for Ichiro - and to see this through."

"Please keep it."

"Take it," he ordered. She put it in her purse.

She turned to look back at him, and there were tears in her eyes. "Thank you, Keith, for Ichiro, for mother, for…" She stopped.

His throat was suddenly dry. "Will you give your mother many kisses for me?"

"Every day, until we meet again."

"Goodbye, Hiroko."

"I love you, Keith."

"And I love you."

She stepped out, leaving the door ajar, and started towards the parking lot where she had left Kimiko's car. Masters got behind the wheel, then put his head out of the window to watch her walking stiffly up the street. She was going to have a long drive tonight, back to Tokyo, to establish her alibi.

He started the car and drove through the town, then out to the countryside for a couple of miles until he reached the next stop. It was a small grove of trees. He turned in and parked.

He helped Ichiro out of the trunk, then picked up his blanket and the one the boy had been lying on. "Come." He led him across an open field to a copse about two hundred yards away, where he spread the blankets. "We'll stay here until it's time to go."

They sat down. The boy was silent for a while. "Hiroko told me how much you care for mother. I feel very bad that you are in so much trouble because of me."

"If I can get you free, your mother will be a happy woman."

"But she will be sad that you have gone."

"Perhaps we may meet again. I'll try to work it out."

Ichiro was silent again. Masters thought he had fallen asleep, but soon he shifted his position. "Lie down and sleep," he told the boy.

"I am not tired," said Ichiro. "Mr. Masters, would you please tell me about my father?"

"What do you want to know?"

"What he was like, when you saw him."

"I don't remember, Ichiro. The fight was over very quickly - and I left soon after. I think I've obtained more of a picture of him since I've been here than from the few minutes - we met."

"Did he die bravely?"

"Yes, but his courage was not just shown in the way he died, but rather in the way he continued the struggle during the weeks when there was no hope. A lesser man would have given up long before then."

"Would you have?"

"Yes."

"That's hard to believe, Mr. Masters."

"Perhaps. But it's true."

The boy was silent again. Then he stirred. "Will you come to North Korea with me?"

"No, I fought them in my lifetime. They are still my enemy."

"You fought my country also."

Masters grinned; this boy was so much like Hiroko. "I said that incorrectly," he acknowledged. "Their ideology is my enemy."

"But you are helping me."

"There are exceptions to everything."

The boy hesitated. "I am not a Communist, Mr. Masters. I never was."

"I figured that. They were the instrument of your hatred, weren't they?"

"Yes."

"Will you mind going to North Korea?"

"No, I want to live."

Speaking of living reminded Masters of something. He counted out several bills and gave them to the boy. "Here's five hundred thousand yen. I guess your mother will get more to you later if you need it."

The boy took the money. "Thank you."

Masters leaned back against a tree, very tired. "Would you," he asked Ichiro, "have used the gun if the guard had moved?"

"No."

"Both of us were in danger."

"I would not have shot him. I could never harm another person, never."

Masters sat up. "Listen to me carefully, Ichiro. You have murdered a man. You've had time to think about it and understand what a terrible thing you've done. But that doesn't mean you shouldn't fight if you have to - if you believe what you're doing is right."

"Would you have shot the guard?"

"You're damned right I would have."

"But we were in the wrong."

"You were, I wasn't. If I had killed him and been put in prison for the rest of my life, or even sentenced to be executed for it, I would still believe that what I had done was right." The boy was confused. "Look, Ichiro, a lot of values in this world of ours are at odds with each other. The Bible says you must not kill, but society declares wars and says, 'Boys, go ahead and kill

- you've got a special dispensation and an up-to-date hunting license'.

"Society says you should not murder, and it has electric chairs and scaffolds and gas tablets to punish those who do. But if someone had murdered Hitler or Tojo or Mussolini, he would have been given a medal. The answer, I guess, is to be with the right society at the right time.

"However, there is another value, that which is within a man himself. What he believes in. Each man has to weigh his own convictions, because in the end he's the one who has to live with them - and maybe die because of them. And somewhere along a man's life, he has to fight. It would be wonderful if the most he had to do was to punch somebody on the nose, but generally it doesn't work out that way. But if he has once burned his fingers and says he will never use fire again because of that, he's running away and, sure as God made apples, the fire will catch up with him.

"You've killed wrongly, and you're trying to atone for it by simply saying you'll never kill again. That's not enough. You've got to try to make amends, by looking around you every day and helping this person and that person and paying it back, dime by dime, even though you know you can never completely repay it.

"And somewhere along the line you may have to fight for this person or that person, because violence is the way of life. But if you turn your back on fighting, then it isn't atonement - it's self-pity. Just make sure, when you turn away, that some innocent person doesn't take the blow meant for you."

He held up his watch to the dim light of the quarter-moon. "We've got to get some rest." They lay down, and soon he heard the boy's even breathing. He put his arms behind his head, and, thinking about Kimiko, he was soon asleep.

Masters woke shortly before 4 a.m. He lay still, wondering what the next few hours and days would bring. When he realized that he was about to build castles in the air, he sat up, stretched, and looked down at the sleeping boy.

At four-thirty he shook him awake, folded the blankets, and led the way back to the car. "Up front," he told him. He started the car, and in a few minutes they were on the road to Naoetsu. He drove slowly, aware that the final stop was only ten minutes away and that he must not arrive before five o'clock.

The small fishing village of Naoetsu was still asleep when they arrived.

He drove directly to the waterfront, then along the dock area to a shed. "Open it," he said.

Ichiro stepped out, opened the door, and stood back as Masters eased the car inside. He could barely get out of the car, the shed was so narrow. He closed the door and led the way along the dock.

Fishermen were stirring, with here and there a boat already putting out to fish the Sea of Japan. He went straight to a small sloop, about thirty feet long, and jumped aboard, motioning to the boy to follow.

An old fisherman with a long, scraggly, gray beard came out of the pilothouse, buttoning his pants. Behind him was a young boy of about sixteen, still half asleep.

"Good morning," said Masters. "Can we get started right away?"

The old man scratched his head and grinned. Masters turned to Ichiro. "I've been having trouble making him understand." The boy immediately passed on the order, and the old man, yawning, nodded his head, went to the auxiliary motor, tinkered with it for a few minutes, and soon it came to life, sounding as if it would not hold up very long.

Masters and Ichiro crowded into the tiny, smelly pilothouse to keep out of sight. In a few minutes, the boat started out to sea. The sun was well up by the time the old man set sail and turned southwest.

When they were far out from land, Masters led Ichiro out on deck. "The old man," he explained, "has been hired to take us to Kangnung, South Korea. That's about seventy-five miles from the Commie border. I told him we were going to South Korea because he would probably be afraid to go anywhere near North Korea. The chart shows that we must sail about a day and a half to reach Kangnung. Tomorrow morning we will make him change direction and go due west, rather than southwest. That will put us in North Korean waters."

He stretched his tired muscles; lack of sleep and anxiety had drained his energy. "Try to find out where he keeps his charts and ask him to explain them to you."

The boy went off, and Masters sat down wearily. A short while later, Ichiro roused him, placing on the deck an old, soiled chart. "He says we will sail generally along this line," the boy said, "and will reach these points every six hours."

Masters blinked the sleep from his eyes and leaned over to study it. "Where will we be tomorrow morning?" he asked.

"Here."

"Okay, we'll force the change of course then. Are you sleepy?"

"No."

"Then keep watch. When you become tired, wake me up." With that, he turned away, rolled himself in the blankets he had brought from the car, and went back to sleep.

At noon, the old man boiled rice and fish, but Masters ate just some rice and drank a bottle of beer. The day passed slowly, finally ebbing away into darkness. They took turns sleeping throughout the night.

At sun-up they faced the old man, "Tell him to change course to due west," ordered Masters. Ichiro translated.

The old man squatted and tugged at his beard. He sat a full minute before he let loose a torrent of words. Ichiro heard him out patiently, then turned to Masters. "He is afraid the North Koreans will confiscate his boat and put him in jail for entering their waters. He refuses to do it."

"Offer him two hundred thousand yen extra. I've already given him seventy-five thousand and promised him one hundred and fifty thousand more when we land at Kangnung."

The old man thought this over for another full minute, then spoke again at great length. "He repeats himself," explained Ichiro, "and adds that this boat is worth much more than that. Also that the North Koreans will take the money from him anyhow."

Masters squatted by the old man, thinking. He had to agree that the fisherman did have a point. "Ask him," he finally said, "if he will sail in close enough to the North Korean coast for you to row his small boat ashore." The rowboat atop the cabin was battered and Masters looked at it apprehensively.

The question threw the old man into a frenzy. "He doesn't want to go near them, under any circumstances," said Ichiro.

"Okay, let's take over," growled Masters. He drew out his pistol and aimed it at the old man. The fisherman just grinned. Masters lowered the weapon and pulled the trigger. The bullet struck a couple of inches away from the old man's foot. He remained squatting, peering at the hole in the deck. Masters fired again at the same spot. The bullet bored in an inch nearer. The man's foot involuntarily turned inward, so Masters quickly fired a third time. It still didn't faze the fisherman.

Masters sighed, then placed a bullet through the fleshy part of the man's upper arm. The old man stared at the blood staining his jacket sleeve, then, still silent, he untied the band of cloth holding up his pants and bound it over the wound.

"Tell him the next one goes right through his head!" snapped Masters.

His tone of voice, rather than the explanation by Ichiro, brought results. The old man muttered something to the boy and stood up. "He agrees," said Ichiro. "But he wants his money now."

Masters counted out one hundred and fifty thousand yen and handed it to the fisherman. "Tell him that he gets the two hundred thousand bonus only when you are put ashore."

For the remainder of the day they watched the man and boy closely, consenting to the changes of course to expend time until nightfall, but taking turns to read the compass and record time and direction to ascertain that the old man was up to no tricks.

Just before darkness fell, the boat, having slowly closed in on North Korea all day, was pointed due west and kept on course. About two o'clock in the morning, they were but a few miles from shore.

"He doesn't want to go any further," said Ichiro.

"Tell him to keep going or I'll pull down the sails and go in myself with the auxiliary engine." The boat kept sailing.

A half-hour later, the old man was in a frenzy again, absolutely refusing to go any further. "He's afraid we might hit something," said the boy.

"Okay." The fisherman and his young assistant dropped the sails, lowered the rowboat over the side, and stood back waiting. Masters led Ichiro to the stern of the sloop. He looked down at him and grinned. "Guess you may make it, son. Take the old man's flashlight. When you get ashore, signal me with two long and two short flashes."

Ichiro shyly put out his hand. "Thank you, Mr. Masters, thank you for my life. And I will not forget anything you have said, ever."

Ichiro and the fisherman's assistant got into the rowboat, and it was quickly swallowed up by the darkness. Masters and the old man squatted by the rail, anxiously watching the shoreline.

It was almost an hour later that he saw two long and then two short flashes. He picked up a flashlight resting beside him and signaled back. Then he handed the flashlight to the old man to guide his assistant back, and stood up.

He knew his body had held out only until this moment, so he didn't fight it any longer. His hand went to his pocket, brought out the bottle of pills, and unscrewed the cap. For a moment he thought he was going to beat it. He got the pill into his mouth. Then it hit! He slumped to his knees as if he had been shot in the chest. He clawed at his jacket and shirt while the screams welled up inside him, then he felt the unbearable agony that put an end to any thought of screaming.

Finally he tumbled to the deck.

CHAPTER 14

Masters later learned that everything in the book had happened that day. First, the old man had dragged his body into the pilothouse, happily concluding that he was dead. He had taken the remainder of the money from Masters' pocket, the equivalent of one thousand two hundred dollars, and debated whether or not to cast him overboard.

Fortunately, Masters had stirred, so the old man had thrown a blanket over him and set sail for Japan. At late afternoon, a Japanese patrol boat had stumbled upon them. The police had initially flung the net southwest, far off the trail, due to the fisherman's grandson, the sixteen-year old boy, having mentioned around the dock that they had a charter for Kangnung, South Korea.

The patrol boat captain, congratulating himself on this chance encounter, had taken the semi-conscious American aboard, put a guard on the old man's boat to keep an eye on things, and had then gunned his twin engines to speed back to his base at Niigata.

They had arrived early the following morning, and the police doctors at Niigata had placed Masters in isolation, giving him merely normal care. A shattering phone call from Tokyo changed all that; they began rushing about to make certain that the pale, clammy American lived long enough to talk.

Ten days later, he was loaded into an ambulance and, with a strong police escort, was taken to Tokyo and lodged in the National Police Hospital.

By this time, Masters had regained sufficient strength to be aware of what was going on around him. He was carried into a room off the main ward, and a guard was stationed at the door. He didn't know why a guard was necessary; the windows were barred and, anyway, he lacked the strength to even crawl off the bed.

They gave him another week before the inquisition began. The door opened and two Japanese entered. One was tall and the other short. The short man stood at the foot of the bed and opened a pad while the tall one came to Masters' side and sat on a white, metal chair.

"We are from the National Police," he said. "You are Keith Masters." It wasn't even a question.

Masters didn't bother answering.

"Are you Keith Masters?" the policeman finally asked.

"Yes."

"Where have you been living since you came to Japan?"

Masters sighed. "I want to talk to somebody from the American Embassy."

"They have been notified of your apprehension. Now, where have you been living?"

"I want to talk to somebody from the American Embassy," repeated Masters.

"They will come when they decide to come. Answer my question."

"I'll wait for them before I say anything."

The cop shrugged and signaled to his partner, who closed his pad and opened the door. Captain Watanabe entered. He came to the foot of the bed and looked at Masters, his unblinking eyes expressing no emotion whatsoever. The lanky man spoke in Japanese, and the Captain answered briefly in a flat tone of voice. Then Watanabe left the room.

Lieutenant Fujii came in next. His eyes were different; they were full of rage. He stood straight as a rod as he answered a few questions then walked stiffly from the room.

The driver of the car which had taken Ichiro from the prison then entered. He replied quietly to the questions. As he turned to leave, Masters said, "I'm sorry."

"Sorry about what?" the tall one asked immediately.

"I was just clearing my throat," said Masters.

The cop didn't have a sense of humor; he motioned to his partner to bring in the guard who had been on the rear seat with Ichiro. He was the one who had been unafraid, and Masters thought he would climb over the foot of the bed at him. He answered the questions loudly and at length and it was evident that he wasn't putting in any good words for the man lying on the bed.

"I'm sorry," said Masters lamely, as the guard turned to go.

He spun round, his lips twisting into a snarl, then he controlled himself and strode out. The tall cop didn't even ask Masters if he had been clearing his throat again.

They brought in the guards from the information desk at the prison, then the two girls and the middle-aged man from Watanabe's outer office, and even the officer who had opened the prison gate to let out the car.

Masters enjoyed the visit of the clerk from the small hotel - or rather he enjoyed the discomfort it gave to the lanky cop. The clerk talked and talked, as if he had kept a day by day diary of Masters' stay there. He understood some of the man's remarks; about a well-dressed woman who drove an expensive car; a beautiful girl who visited his room almost every day; the way his bed was never mussed up by sleeping or - he became dramatic - love-making; and on and on and on.

The cop must have heard all this before, for he tried several times to interrupt, but without success, so he fidgeted until the clerk ran out of words.

After the talkative one had left, they brought in a bespectacled man, who was identified as a clerk from the second hotel, then the people from the car rental agencies, and later on a few more he had never seen before, or did not recall seeing.

The old fisherman came in carrying his arm in a sling, and he immediately began talking faster than the first hotel clerk, pointing to his injured arm and going through all sorts of gestures for the benefit of the police taking the report. Masters wondered how much he would try to sue him for, since the minor flesh wound would keep growing and growing until it became a permanent disability.

The young boy from the boat was next, and after him came a clerk from one of the stores where he had tried to purchase a handgun.

Then suddenly, the room was empty, and he lay back, sighing with relief. He should have known better, for the tall cop reappeared, and with him was Lieutenant Colonel Charles Durkin.

The Colonel looked closely at Masters, then turned to the police investigator. "He's the one," he said, simply.

"Can I speak to him - alone?" asked Masters.

The cop thought this over, then nodded. When he had gone, Masters cocked an eye at Durkin. "I guess you understand why I can't say anything for the record, but if I could, I would say I'm sorry."

For a moment the Colonel wasn't certain how to treat it, then he relaxed. "I've gotten a few of the facts together," he said, "and from what I've heard, I might be tempted to forgive you. Incidentally, I received all my personal effects by mail a couple of weeks ago. I can see it wasn't robbery." He hesitated. "I had to tell the police about getting them back. But last week I received a very beautiful set of jade earrings - for my wife, I guess. Should I say anything?"

Masters shook his head. That damned Hiroko. "Are you okay?" he asked.

"That crack on the head? I'm all right - it didn't kill me. But it sure played hell with my reputation. I was a judo instructor for five years, and now I'll have to quit bragging. Well, so long, Masters, I hope they're not too rough on you."

And that took care of the morning.

In the afternoon, he was barraged by the Americans. Directly after lunch, an alert looking young fellow came in. "Mr. Masters?" he asked, cheerfully.

"Yes."

"I'm Pete McMahon, of the Embassy. Would have gotten down to see you before now, but they said you were still somewhat under the weather."

They shook hands. "Glad to see you," said Masters, relieved. He eyed the young man. "What's the land of the Great White Father going to do?"

"Oh, we'll be there with you. I'd better explain right off the bat that you are definitely subject to Japanese law, but we'll see that you get proper legal representation. Do you have any money?"

"Not a helluva lot."

"Well, you can be sure your rights will be protected and that you will be assigned a proper attorney by the State. He may not be first class, as the Japanese Government have a list and one is selected by lot, but we'll have someone from the Embassy attend the trial and see that everything is according to law and all that."

"And then what?"

The young fellow caught the gleam of humor in Masters' eyes. "Well, after they sentence you to a couple of hundred years in prison, we'll come by now and then. By the way, do you need anything?"

"Yeah, how about getting somebody to break me out of here?"

They both laughed. "Sorry we can't help more," added McMahon, "but your treatment will be quite above board, we'll see to that."

"How about bail?"

"We've already checked on that. It was refused."

Masters felt much better after the enthusiastic young man had left; at least he wouldn't be getting a drum-head trial.

A short while later, there was a knock at the door, and Bill Wilson, accompanied by a tall, gray-haired full Colonel, came in. Bill tried to hide his anxiety with a big grin, but it didn't come off too well. He shook Masters' hand.

"Hi, you wild bastard," he said, rather softly. "I should have known you were up to something. Are you all right?"

"I'm okay, Bill. Thanks. Did they grill you?"

"And how. What a patsy you made of me. The Old Man is eyeing me like I should have my head examined." He turned to the Colonel. "Sir, this is Keith Masters. Keith, this is Colonel Carradine. I hope you don't mind my bringing him along."

Masters glanced at the Judge Advocate's insignia on his uniform. "Is the United States Army going to hang me, too?"

The Colonel grinned as he brought a chair over to the bed. "Hello, Masters," he said, shaking his hand. "Wilson has been beating my ear off, so I thought I'd come along and have a few words with you." He pulled out a folder. "We sent to Washington for your record. You've been a pretty good soldier."

"Pretty good, my eye," interjected Bill. "He was a real soldier. Christ, Colonel, we just can't let the Nips drop him into one of their cells."

"Your record," explained the Colonel, "would have weight in an American court, but the Japanese..." He glanced again at the folder. "A Silver Star with cluster..."

"One of those Silver Stars was mine," interrupted Bill. "He wouldn't have gotten it without me."

"Lay off," said Masters.

"Like hell, I will," replied Bill, seriously. "I owe you one, Keith, a real big one. You just shut up and let people say what they must." He turned to the Colonel. "Keith saved my life in Korea, and not by just reaching out a hand and pulling a fellow back into a hole. Colonel, I don't give a shit what he's done, you've got to help."

"Well, perhaps it would be best to get all the facts before giving an opinion."

Masters sat up a little. "If I say anything, can they make you reveal it in court?"

Carradine rubbed his jaw. "They can work on Wilson, but I can claim a consultant's immunity." He turned to Bill. "How about taking a walk?"

"Okay," he replied, pleased to see that the Colonel intended to help. "I'll wait outside."

Masters told the Colonel the entire story, from start to finish, from Iwo Jima to Kimiko's house. He left out nothing except intimate details. The officer listened closely, making notes every now and then. When

Masters had finished, he leaned back in his chair and rocked to and fro for a few minutes.

"Well," he finally said. "There isn't a damn thing the United States Government can do to you. Your only concern is the Japanese court, and I'm not enough of an expert in their law to advise you."

"You mean I haven't violated American law? How about wearing the uniform?"

"The impersonation of an officer was not done in the United States."

"How about conking Durkin and taking his things?"

"The housing area was on property subject to Japanese law. Even if we had caught you in the act, we would still have had to turn you over to them. You're a civilian. The army has no jurisdiction over you, and the United States civil authorities have none either - as regards this case. You can only be tried and sentenced by the people having jurisdiction, and in this action it is the Japanese. Of course, if you ever return to the United States, Colonel Durkin could bring suit for physical damages, if any were sustained. Outside of that - nothing." He called in Bill. "There's nothing for me here, Wilson. Masters has not violated any American law."

Bill heaved a great sigh of relief. "How about the Nip courts. Can you help there?"

"I'll speak to some of my people in the office and look for a good attorney. They come high, though."

"Don't worry about that," said Wilson.

"Bill…" started Masters.

"No dice," said Bill, cutting him off short. "You just lie quiet and rest." He took Masters' hand. "Hold on tight, wild man. I'll visit you again as soon as I get something going."

When they had gone, he lay back and tried to calm his jumping heart. They wouldn't get him to court alive if the door kept opening and closing like it did today. He tried to think of Kimiko, but he was too weary. He was too weary to think of anything except breaking down and crying, and maybe begging to be put some place where it was restful, where the vise-like pressure on his chest could be eased.

For a moment he thought of Ichiro, of when the boy had asked him if he would have surrendered, and how he had said "yes". But deep inside, he knew he was pulling the kid's leg, that he would have tried to kill at least one more guy instead of hiding in a cave and rotting away like a vegetable.

But now he wanted to surrender, and didn't know how. All he wanted was peace and quiet, for people to leave him alone so he could get that goddamn weight off his chest and that crummy, broken-down heart to allay its searing pain.

But he could feel the net drawing in relentlessly. They were going to stamp on him, cut him up, hurt and torture his body - and all the praying and begging and blustering in the world wouldn't make one goddamn bit of difference. If it hurt one iota more, he decided, I'd kill myself. Then I'd have no more of it. But like some gullible simpleton, my brain will listen to some fool nonsense that the pain and heaviness inside must sooner or later ease up and will tell the muscles not to finish me off yet, but to hold off for just a little longer. Horseshit.

He tried to sleep that night, but it was difficult to go under, and it was a restless sleep that weakened the already fragile fibers of his heart.

In the morning, the doctor took one look at him and stopped all further questioning. It was three more days before the police could prevail upon him to relax his restrictions, and on the following morning, Masters got his first pleasant surprise. Mr. Takahashi, Ichiro's attorney, walked in. He stopped at the doorway, bowed, and advanced to the bed. Behind him was a tall, husky, young man. Without a word, the lawyer reached into an inner pocket and handed Masters a sealed envelope. Masters motioned for them to take seats, then tore open the envelope. It was a letter from Hiroko.

'Oh, Keith, dear, dear Keith. Mother and I are frantic with worry. We hope you are getting better, and we send our love and our gratitude. Please, Keith, keep well for us. Mother has sent Mr. Takahashi to assist you. He is very interested in your case. Will you please accept him? Just nod at him. He'll understand.'

Masters raised his eyes to the lawyer and nodded. Takahashi nodded back and placed one finger in the palm of his other hand.

'With Mr. Takahashi,' continued Hiroko, 'is Mr. Kawamoto, his chief assistant, who speaks fluent English and can interpret. Mr. Kawamoto is a wonderful young man. He told me to shut up and keep to the point when I spoke about you. He looks and acts so much like you that I think I could fall in love with him. Please nod again at Mr. Takahashi if you accept him as an interpreter.'

Masters studied the tall, husky aide. Like hell he looks like me; that fellow is a damned good-looking guy. He switched his glance to the attorney and nodded again. Takahashi placed a second finger in his palm.

'Keith, mother and I are determined to visit you. Mr. Takahashi says we should not, but he is only smart in legal matters. Now you just nod 'yes' at him.'

Masters grinned and shook his head. The lawyer almost smiled, then took his fingers out of his hand.

The next part of the letter was written in tiny, precise letters, and they reminded him immediately of the woman.

'My dear Keith. Forgive me, dear husband, for having had doubts during the weeks you were worrying and making yourself ill to help Ichiro. Thank you, dear husband, for having given life back to my son. My heart is sad that you are not a free man and that you have no one to take care of you. I have been to my altar and prayed like I have never prayed before. I love you.' It was signed, 'Kimiko, your wife.'

Masters folded the letter and began to place it under the pillow to be reread at a later time, but Takahashi reached out and plucked it from his hand.

"The Honorable Counsel for the Defense, Mr. Takahashi," said the young man, in a clear, firm voice, "wishes to retain the epistle until a more appropriate time. It contains material which should not be revealed to the prosecution." Masters nodded.

"The Honorable Counsel…" Takahashi must have caught the drift, for he waved a hand, and Kawamoto got down to business. "Please, Mr. Masters, would you tell Mr. Takahashi all the details. I am to inform you that Mrs. Tanaka has spoken at great length regarding her relationship with you, and her daughter, Miss Tanaka, has recounted every incident of which she is cognizant. You may exclude, if you wish, all information leading up to your arrival in Japan, such as the battle on Iwo Jima, and," he hesitated, swallowed, and continued, "any personal facts relating to yourself or to Mrs. Tanaka."

Masters grinned to himself; Hiroko would eat this boy up. Then he sobered down and began the story all over again. Kawamoto was a good translator. He spoke lucidly, without hesitation, and seemed to express Masters' sentiments exactly. It took a long time, and now and then Takahashi interrupted to recheck a point or to ask a question. He made no notes.

When Masters had finished, the attorney sat quietly, turning the details over in his mind. Then Masters learned why Kimiko had engaged him. Kawamoto translated as if Mr. Takahashi himself were speaking.

"Mr. Masters, you are guilty of the following violations of Japanese law; you have assaulted Colonel Durkin with a deadly weapon, inflicted a wound upon him, and committed armed robbery. The wounding of the officer will not be a serious charge, as he has fully recovered. Furthermore, the charge could be fought on the grounds of common assault.

"You have entered the American Post Exchange and purchased military supplies. That does not violate the Status-of-Forces agreement, nor does the wearing of the uniform constitute a felony, regardless of its purpose. You have, however, bought an attaché case. That violates the Status-of-Forces agreement in that you have purchased this article without having paid customs and sales tax on it. The government will insist upon this." Masters almost laughed.

"Your impersonation as an officer of the United States Army at the prison is without precedent, and the prosecution would be amiss in bringing this charge against you. Your deceiving of Captain Watanabe and Lieutenant Fujii is merely interference with the police, and is a misdemeanor. This is an offense of secondary importance.

"The freeing of a prisoner is obstruction of justice, and is a serious charge. The striking of the two guards is assault with a lethal weapon, and is a much more serious offense than the assault against the American officer, as the police were acting in the performance of their duty.

"The renting of vehicles and the purchasing of the pistols do not break the law. However, if there is damage to the cars, the companies can, and will, seek indemnity.

"The wounding of the owner of the boat is again assault with a lethal weapon, and the forcing of the boat to sail for North Korea is piracy, for you did, in essence, assume command by force. However, as he did ask for money and did accept one hundred and fifty thousand yen after the assault, and then did change course, you can disregard any action against you. He cannot even sue you for injuries sustained, as the one hundred and fifty thousand yen is evidence of his having accepted compensation for the wound, and agreeing, for an additional sum of two hundred thousand yen, to the change in course. Your statement about taking the vessel in by the auxiliary engine can be construed as having been a disagreement as to the distance inshore stipulated in your contract.

"You will receive four years of imprisonment for the assault with an offensive weapon upon Colonel Durkin, two months for interference with the duties of the police, eight years for the obstruction of justice in having freed a prisoner, and eleven years for assault with a lethal weapon upon the guards who were acting in the performance of their duty. This comes to a total of twenty-three years and two months.

"Appeals will consume approximately two years, and at the conclusion, the sentence will be reduced to approximately thirteen years. You will then be eligible for parole in eight years."

He rose. "Do you have any questions, Mr. Masters?" There were none; Masters was almost in a state of shock. The attorney bowed, then thrust out his hand for an American handshake.

Lester Taube

CHAPTER 15

Masters did not sleep very much that night, so when the tall police investigator and his short partner entered the room the following morning, he was in a morose and contrary mood.

"Have you anything further to say?" asked the lanky cop.

A devil took hold of the weary man. "You're damn right I have," he snarled. The investigator leaned forward eagerly, the short one whipping out his notebook and pencil. "I wish to state publicly," said Masters, in a clear, firm voice, "that the information you have obtained from the people you paraded through here is absolutely correct." The tall man almost smiled. "Furthermore, I also wish to state publicly that Ichiro Tanaka's escape was engineered with the full cooperation and approval of high-ranking police officers and officials of the Japanese government, and that I was brought to Japan for the express purpose of carrying out that plan. I will not tolerate being double-crossed, and will reveal all identities at my trial."

He lay back and closed his eyes - but not before he saw the look of utter stupefaction on the face of the tall agent. He lay in the deepest silence he had ever experienced, then there was the sound of footsteps and the opening and closing of the door. He raised an eyelid and saw that the room was empty.

The deluge swept in less than an hour later. Captain Watanabe and Lieutenant Fujii were the first ones. The Captain's eyes were not expressionless this time; they were flashing flames of outraged fury. Fujii's face was a mask of absolute hatred. They shouted, yelled, stamped their feet, threatened, jerked at the bed, pushed over chairs, and almost reached the point of laying hands on the bed-ridden man. Masters kept his eyes closed and refused to open them or to reply. Watanabe's voice finally gave out half an hour later and they went away.

McMahon, from the United States Embassy, must have been waiting outside. He tramped in and stood stiffly at attention. "Are you trying to create an international incident?" he roared. Masters was tempted to ask him whatever had happened to his collegiate manners, but remained silent and shut his eyes instead.

He didn't open his eyes but he did listen carefully to the next visitor. "Mr. Masters," said a soft voice. "I am from the Japanese Ministry of State. My office would look with great favor upon you if you would kindly reveal the names of the people who have participated in this plot. I am quite confident that our appreciation would be demonstrated in court."

Masters opened his eyes and saw a small, well-dressed man, his hat resting squarely on his head, seated on one of the white, metal chairs at the foot of the bed. He closed his eyes. The man sat quietly until he realized that Masters would not speak, then left the room.

The next visitor was from the Ministry of Justice and offered even more for the names - merely five years in prison. Masters did not bother to open his eyes to look.

Then the flood stopped; he was cut off from the outside world. For three days, the only people who entered his room were the doctor and the attendant who brought his meals. Each was escorted by a guard who made certain that Masters did not pass a message to the hospital personnel.

On the fourth day, the well-dressed man from the Ministry of State returned. "Mr. Masters," he said, in his soft voice. "I am sure you understand the gravity of the charges against you. Would you please not reconsider?"

Masters opened his eyes. The visitor's hat was still squarely on his head. "Go discuss it with Mr. Takahashi," he ordered, then closed his eyes again.

Mr. Takahashi and his assistant, Kawamoto, were there directly after lunch.

The lawyer was smiling.

"I have," translated his assistant, "been visited this morning by a number of government officials, who informed me of the statement you gave to the investigating officers. Before we go any further, I wish to advise you categorically that I do not want to know whether the statement is true or not." His smile grew broader. "All the officials are convinced that you are lying, but they have asked me to intercede."

"So," mused Masters. "Politics are the same the world over." He glanced up at Kawamoto. "What have the newspapers been saying?"

The young man spoke to the attorney and was given permission to reply. "They have been filled with the most inaccurate stories about Tanaka's escape, and the capture of an American who engineered it. Your identity has not yet been revealed to the public, and I am certain that the police have sworn all participants to strict silence. The news media of the center left and the center right are hinting at a complicity between the present administration and certain unidentified parties. The center right infers that it is a Communist plot, and the center left intimates that the far right is in collusion with the government."

Masters whistled softly. "Then perhaps we can fish in troubled waters, eh?"

The young man's eyes were shining. "Yes."

Masters turned back to the attorney. "What do the officials want?"

"They are willing," translated Kawamoto, "to have the prosecution recommend ten years of imprisonment as a sentence and permit me to appeal. It should end up with no more than five years of actual confinement." He regarded Masters closely. "They wish, however, to have the names first, undoubtedly to take immediate action to silence the rumors being bandied about by their political opponents." Takahashi raised a brow. "If there are names. However, if there are no names, they want you to make a full confession to dispel the doubt."

Masters lay back, the excitement was taxing his heart. He was suddenly very weary again. "I'll think it over," he said.

Takahashi saw his condition, bowed, and prepared to leave. Kawamoto leaned over closer. "Hiroko..." He caught himself. "Miss Tanaka gave me this message for you. Mr. 0 has written. He is well and working in a factory."

Masters nodded, then closed his eyes. It had worked. He had given the boy his life in exchange for the one he had taken from the father. Nothing else really mattered - not really.

Keith Masters reached a decision two days later, shouted for the guard at the door, and asked to see Takahashi. The attorney and his aide were there in almost no time. "I want a package deal," said Masters. "Me and Ichiro, together." The lawyer sat up, and Masters continued, "Our main objective is to help the boy - so that he does not have to continue running or remain in exile for the rest of his life. Have them consider this; if the boy returns voluntarily, it will take the wind out of the sails of the opposition who are saying that the escape was engineered by the Government. Ask them what they will give in return. If it is acceptable, I will reveal the names they want, and promise to remain silent in the courtroom - and afterwards."

They almost ran from the room. It must have been quite a bargaining session, for they did not return until nightfall, and their faces were drawn with fatigue. Kawamoto could not control his eagerness to speak.

"The officials acquiesce. Tanaka's sentence will be commuted to life imprisonment. Your sentence will be as last proposed - about five years actual confinement."

Masters did not hesitate. "Tell them the whole deal is off, that I am ordering my attorney to release my statement to the newspapers."

Takahashi sighed, for obtaining the commutation was more than he had hoped for. Courteously, he asked one question. "What would Mr. Masters consider as a basis for negotiation?"

"Twenty years for Ichiro, no more. After all, he doesn't <u>have</u> to return. And twenty years is a lifetime to a young boy. I don't give a damn about myself. They can set their own limit on that."

The accidence came so swiftly that it caught the lawyer, Kawamoto, and even Masters off balance. Takahashi explained that the rumors had grown to such an extent that the administration was now completely on the defensive.

"Do you have a water-tight agreement?" asked Masters. "No loopholes?"

The lawyer smiled. "No loopholes."

Masters sighed in relief, then a thought suddenly struck him. "I've forgotten one thing - you must ask Mrs. Tanaka if she agrees."

"I already have."

"What did she say?"

"She said that the head of the house must decide."

"All right. Have Hiroko write to Ichiro right away and find out if he accepts."

The attorney's eyes softened. "She was not referring to Ichiro," he said.

It took a few seconds for this to register, then Masters' heart began thumping again, but not from pain. "Very well, have Hiroko write and tell him to return," he said finally.

The October winds were sweeping the streets. Masters stood at the barred window, looking out at the cloud-filled sky. He was fully dressed and wearing a fine overcoat which Takahashi had brought. He knew it had come from Kimiko. The door opened to admit two guards. One walked up to him and held out handcuffs. Masters raised his right arm and the cold steel encircled his wrist. They went out into the corridor, took an elevator down the three flights of stairs, and entered a police van. Masters drew his coat tighter against the cold.

The courthouse was packed. The cuff was taken off, and he was escorted to a long table at the front of the room. Takahashi and Kawamoto were already there. They rose and bowed as he took his seat. His eyes flicked over the assembly seated to the rear. Kimiko and Hiroko were not there. He had given strict instructions for them not to attend, but deep inside he had hoped they would come anyhow, for he wanted to see them so badly. He knew Kimiko would obey, but he felt that Hiroko was enough of a rascal to come, regardless of his order.

He didn't look for the officials who had bombarded him during his hectic weeks in the hospital. He almost chuckled at the memory of the last meeting with them, when all the secret papers had been signed, sealed and delivered. They had crowded into his room and stood there, expectantly, to hear the names.

"There are none," he had said, simply. "I was lying."

They had not even become angry. In fact, he sensed a wave of relief sweep over them. Then, after the officials had left, the tall investigator and his partner had come in and taken down all the details which Masters had refused earlier. He did not mention his personal associations with Kimiko, nor did he speak of Hiroko, and the officers did not try to clear up certain points which evidently required the assistance of an accomplice. He realized that the tall man was aware of these gaps and had been ordered to cooperate.

The court action was over by early afternoon. They called only Fujii, the two guards whom he had assaulted, and the old fisherman. They must have worked over the old man, for he had very little to say. The sentence followed swiftly on the heels of the verdict - Takahashi had gauged it to a hair - they gave him thirteen years confinement with hard labor.

When the guards came to take him away, the attorney stood and bowed. Then, as he had done once before, he thrust out his hand in the American manner. "Goodbye, my friend," he said.

They took him back to his old room in the National Police Hospital, and the doctor immediately came in to check him over. He couldn't get an injection into Masters' arm fast enough.

He later learned that it had been a rather hectic week. A couple of specialists had been called in, an oxygen tent had been quickly set up, and a flock of nurses had been placed around him - as if he was some goddamn pasha.

In late November, they permitted him to get to his feet, and he finally began to stop wishing that he had died during his last attack so the pain inside would go away.

Fujii came for him in the middle of December. He stood in the doorway, still and straight, and behind him were two guards from the prison. There was a hard glint in the adjutant's eyes. All right, you bastard, thought Masters. Now you get your pound of flesh.

One of the guards placed his clothes on the bed. "Get dressed," snarled Fujii. Masters had to sit on a chair to put on his shoes, and when he leaned forward to tie the laces, he thought he'd still beat the bastard and die on the spot.

Fujii snapped on the handcuffs himself, then tugged on them as he led Masters from the room. One of the guards picked up his suitcase and brought it along. They went down the elevator and got into a police car, which seemed to be the one that was used to take Ichiro from the prison. He wondered if he could be assigned to the same cell as Ichiro. He'd like that. But it would never happen, not with that vindictive bastard, Fujii, running things.

He didn't come awake until he saw the road signs pointing to Yokohama. "Where are we going?" he asked.

"Be quiet," growled the adjutant. Masters was tempted to ask why he was so damned mad; he was going to have thirteen long years to vent his spite. Instead, he looked wistfully out of the window.

The police car drove through Yokohama and stopped at the docks. Fujii jerked him out of the car, literally dragged him to a building, and through it to a counter. He pulled out Masters' passport and handed it to an official to be stamped.

Masters' heart almost stopped beating. Fujii towed him out of the building and to the open quay. A small ship was tied up alongside the pier.

At the gangplank, the adjutant, his face reflecting absolute hatred and disgust, drew out a key and unlocked the handcuffs. He gave Masters' passport to one of the guards following him, then turned to the white faced man.

"The Government of Japan find your physical disability incompatible with the execution of your sentence, and hereby expel you from this country." Then he spat on the ground and walked away.

Sweat was pouring down Masters' face and body as he slowly mounted the gangplank. The guard handed his valise and passport to a steward, then took up a position on the wharf to see that the deportee left with the ship.

The Japanese steward led him to a small cabin, deposited the bag on a rack, and left. Masters sat limply on the lower berth, head spinning, unable to realize that he was a free man.

After a while, he became aware of the wetness of his body, and rose. Slipping out of the overcoat, he placed it on the single chair in the cabin, laid his jacket over it, and hung his sweat-drenched shirt on the corner of the double bunk. He sat down and took off his pants and shoes, flinging them on the jacket.

He had to rest before he could build up the energy to stand and open the valise. On top was the blue, silk robe that Kimiko had given him. It was wrinkled, as if the suitcase had been searched and researched a dozen times. He draped it over his shoulders and sank back on the bunk, breathing heavily, harshly.

There was a knock at the door. "Come in," he said, his voice weak with weariness.

The door opened. He sat silent for a long second. "Hello, Kimiko."

"Hello, Keith," She motioned, and two porters rushed in, carrying a small mountain of fine, handmade luggage. They deposited the bags neatly to one side, bowed several times to acknowledge the tips they received, then quickly left.

Her eyes could not meet his. To look at him, loving him so, would spell the utter collapse of her control. Desperately she glanced round the cabin. "It is too small," she said. "There is not enough room for you to walk around. I will speak to the captain in the morning." He knew she would, too.

Her eyes settled on his clothes lying on the chair. Quickly she walked to the closet, hung up her overcoat, then picked up his pants and folded them neatly over a hanger. She put his jacket over the pants, and hung them next to her coat.

"Where are your pills?" she asked, her back to him. He could see that she was crying.

"In my pocket."

"Put them on the stand so I can see them."

"All right." He placed them on the stand.

She began unpacking his suitcase and stowing away his clothes.

"This boat is going to America," he finally said. "There are no actors in dragon masks there."

"They are not important," she replied, firmly. "Anyhow, Mr. Takahashi said that I should write him in two years - that doors always reopen."

She still could not look at him. She saw his shoes and picked them up, looked around for polishing materials, then laid them to one side. "You should lie down and rest," she said.

He lowered himself on the bunk and placed his hands under his head, watching her every movement.

Her eyes fastened on his shirt hanging on the berth. She took it down, looked at the collar, then carried it to the basin in the corner and turned on the water. It spurted out, splashing her perfectly tailored suit, but she ignored it. She filled the basin and began to soap the shirt, to wash out the sweat and the dirt - like the country women did. She was crying again.

Then she began humming. Masters closed his eyes and listened. "What's that you're humming?"

"It is an old Japanese song. A love song."

He leaned further back on the pillow and felt his body relax. "It's nice. I like it."

"Then I'll hum it," she whispered, "every day of our lives."

Suddenly, she heard a sound - like the flutter of a dove's wings as it takes off and soars skyward. Slowly she turned, wiped her hands on her skirt and walked to the berth. She drew up the chair and sat down, then reached out and gently closed the lids over the staring eyes. She lifted the lifeless arm, hanging limply against the side of the bunk, and laid it across his chest. Then, with infinite tenderness, she kissed his still lips.

When all this had been done, she leaned back in her chair and closed her eyes.

EPILOGUE

Mount Suribachi still loomed high over Iwo Jima. Far below, at the northern tip of the island, two men assisted a woman down through a draw in the precipice to the sands below. Two others lowered a small rubber boat down to them. Carrying the boat, the two men followed the woman along the beach to where an arm of the cliff curved into the sea. They helped her step into the boat, then one of them rowed it around the bend.

"Wait back there," said Kimiko, as she stepped ashore. She drew her coat more tightly around herself, and faced the winds blowing from the sea, feeling the cold of the winter bite through her clothes, matching the chill in her heart. In one hand was a small, exquisite urn.

Then she turned and slowly walked up to the cave. The stone wall had fallen, was covered by the sweeping sands, and the cave looked so much smaller than Masters had described it.

She sank to her knees and she wept, rocking in the time-old ritual of mourning, raising her head between sobs so that she could breathe.

Finally she set down the urn, and dug her hands into the sand, slowly and tenderly opening the grave for the middle-aged man with the cropped hair and light blue eyes. When it was deep enough, she placed the urn in the hole and, equally slowly and tenderly, smoothed the sand over it. Then she turned to stare out over the cold, gray waters, sensing in its relentless, undulating rhythm a kinship with the emptiness within her.

The shadows were lengthening when one of the men rowed around the point. "Mrs. Masters," he called. "We must be getting back. It will be dark soon."

Wearily she rose, turned to look once more at the cave and the smooth patch of sand, then she entered the boat.

Had she dug a few inches more to one side, she would have touched the outstretched fingers of Ito, reaching out across the many years.

The wheel had turned full circle.

END

ABOUT THE AUTHOR

Lester Taube was born of Russian and Lithuanian immigrants in Trenton, New Jersey. He began soldering while in his teens, first in the horse artillery, then as an infantryman for the remainder of his career. In World War II, he was a platoon leader in the Bismark Archipelago, attached to the Marines on Iwo Jima, then on Okinawa, the last battle of the war. Recuperating from wounds and malaria, he left the army to run a 400 employee electronic company in California, a 450 employee paper stock company in Pennsylvania and then moved to Canada to open a logging and pulp-wood cutting operation. Returning to military service, he served as an advisor to the Turkish army, as an intelligence officer and company commander in Korea, then left to become an insurance consultant.

During the Vietnam period, he was stationed in Europe as a general staff officer working in intelligence and war plans. While there, he opened a chain of coin-operated laundries in France that would become the largest in Europe. Prior to retirement as a full colonel, he moved to a small village in Austria and kept a boat for several years in the Cote d'Azur.

Returning to the U.S. after 13 years overseas, he worked as an economic development specialist for the State of New Jersey until his final retirement. He has four children all born in different countries.

Since retirement, he has spent winters in Florida, summers in New Jersey, fished, boated and traveled to

Europe each year, especially to Spain to keep up with his great interest in bull fighting.

He began writing action novels while in France, and after producing four books which were published in a number of different countries, and selling two for motion pictures, he stopped—"as there were children to raise and soldiering to do."